WHO DREW THE TWO?

WHO DREW THE TWO?

MELTON LUTTRELL

ARPress
45 Dan Road Suite 5
Canton MA 02021
Hotline: 1(888) 821-0229
Fax: 1(508) 545-7580

Ordering Information:

Quantity sales. Special discounts are available on quantity purchases by corporations, associations, and others. For details, contact the publisher at the address above.

Printed in the United States of America.
ISBN-13:   Softcover   979-8-89330-900-3

             eBook   979-8-89330-902-7

             Hardback   979-8-89330-901-0

Library of Congress Control Number: 2024902518

Contents

Authors Note

This is my first endeavor to tell a story that is somewhat true, but enhanced with imagination. Some locations in the story are real places that I have knowledge of, having grown up in that general area. However, the characters in this book are totally fictional as well as the basis for the murder in this small town in Texas.

I was inspired to write this story because, now at the age of ninety-two, I have enjoyed reading many Murder-Mystery books, and often wondered if I had the ability, and time required, to write a story of my own. As a kid growing up in a small West Texas town, I experienced some of the events described in this book.

Retired from my day job, but still working several nights a week, I found little time to pursue a writing project. It was sometime in 2010 that I wrote the first chapter, and like most of the book, was written from midnight until around 2:30 in the morning. After writing several chapters, I completely dropped my project, largely because of my wife's failing health.

Susia Mae, my beautiful, faithful, and best friend and wife for sixty-eight plus years, was called to be with our Lord in December of 2015. She was my greatest supporter and the primary reason for any success that I may have achieved in my lifetime.

Late in the year 2020, I picked up the book that I had partially written and read it through several times before deciding to continue to write. In those few years, my typing skills had diminished to the point that I mostly relied on my computer's dictation feature to complete this project.

For one reason or another, it required a lot of backing up, deleting, and one finger typing to finally reach the end.

A big THANK YOU goes to several of my friends and family that furnished valuable detail information regarding hunting, rifles, oil field investments, production and maintenance.

My Sons, Mike and Mark Luttrell: Rifles, Hunting, Fishing, and Football.

My Minister and Dear Friend, Reverend Raul Gutierrez: Revealing events in his father's journey to become a Minister in the United States that I used to describe Pablo's life.

My Cousin, Jerry Lowrance: Oil Production and Leasing.

And the person, more than anyone else, that spent endless hours, by telephone, teaching me computer basics, reviewing spacing, indenting, restoring one or more pages that I had foolishly deleted, and other problems too many to mention:

A Best Friend, Al Frazier: Computer Support.

Thank You to all that take the time to read my novel.

—Melton Luttrell

Biography of Characters: *Who Drew the Two?*

- **ROBERT WILSON (BOB OR BULL) BULLOCK:** Banker
  Wife: Melba Lou
  Secretary: Margaret Ann Burke
- **JIM (WHISTLER) WILLIAMS:** High School Football Coach
  Wife: Mary Josephine
- **BERN WHITLOCK:** Basketball Coach and Assistant
  Football Coach
  Wife: Betty Jo
- **GAIL PRITCHARD:** Owner and operator of Gail's Diner
- **MALCOLM (MAL) MORRIS:** Rancher's Best Friend Feed
  Store Owner
  Brother: Phillip Morris
- **PARKER COBURN:** Owner Of Coburn Oil & Gas
  Wife: Mary Marilyn Martin
  Secretary: Betty Jean Morrison
  Secretary: Mary Francis
  Geologist Employee: Paul Hicks
  Employee and Private Eye: Sandy Smith
- **JOHN JOSEPH (JJ) STEPHENS:** Rancher
  Father: Billy Joe Stephens, Jr.
  Grandfather: Billy Joe Stephens, Sr.
  Ranch Hands: Mannie Garcia, Francisco Gonzales,
  and son Luis

- **PABLO RODRIGUEZ:** Owner Of Pablo's Mexican Cuisine Restaurant
  Wife: Rita
  Daughter: Rose Marie
- **BETTY JEAN (BET) MORRISON:** Secretary To Parker Coburn, wife of Bob Herring Jr.
- **CHAT CASON:** Manager of The Double D Ranching Enterprises
  Wife: Joan Elizabeth (Joanie) Atkins
  Children: Cindi, and Carly
- **ROBERT HERRING, SR.:** Retired Owner Of The Herring Ranch
  Wife: Lillian
  Son: Robert Herring, Jr.
- **ROBERT HERRING JR.:** President Of The Herring Ranch Company
  Wife: Melinda Martin
  Wife: Betty Jean Morrison
  Daughters: Emily Jean and Brenda Kaye
  Ranch Hands: Roy and Jimbo
- **BUCKNER (BUCK) JONES:** Sheriff
  Deputy Sheriff: Randy Spears
  Secretary: Shirley Johnson
- **Ward Thompson:** Burson Police Chief
  Police Officer: Phil Hawkins
- **JEFF FIDLER:** Contract Painter
  Wife and Assistant: Nancy Lee

CHAPTER ONE

A Spring Morning In Burson, Texas, 1984

"Morning Maggie," the warm and usual greeting from Bull Bullock, echoed through the hallway in the small back entrance to the West Texas First National Bank in Burson, Texas. It was a beautiful April morning; and spring was in full bloom in this bustling small town seated in the ranching country a hundred or so miles west of the Ft. Worth/Dallas metroplex. Margaret Ann Burke, affectionately called Maggie by her many friends and fellow employees, jumped to her feet, poured a cup of steaming coffee, added one sugar packet, one small spoon of powdered cream, stirred vigorously, and, as she had done repeatedly for the past twenty years, followed Bull into his private office with the Morning Edition of the Ft. Worth Star Telegram in one hand and the coffee in the other.

Once inside the office, Maggie sat the coffee down on a maroon Texas A&M coaster on Bull's desk, unfolded the paper and placed it in front of his chair and as usual, commenced with the morning small talk. "How was your weekend, Bull? Slay a lot of dragons?"

"Nope . . . nothing significant took place this weekend; just the usual, trying to catch up with the weeds. Gosh almighty, seems as if they grow bigger and faster each year more than the one before. Damned if I can figure out why someone down in Aggie Land can't come up with a kind of grass that will complete eliminate weeds all together. I think I'll just write somebody down there and let them know my annual donation, which is pretty dang generous, is coming to a screeching halt if they don't come up with something pretty quick to take care of these West Texas lawns."

"Well Helloooo Bull," the deliberate mocking reply from Maggie. "As your assistant, I just happen to have access to your personal check ledger, and I would say that you are more than generous to your alma mater. In fact, and as far as I'm concerned, you're way too generous. How about cutting down on that donation and sending a generous portion of that to Maggie's foundation, called How to Keep a Single, Hard-Working Underpaid, Dedicated Employee with no Boyfriends Fed, Clothed, and Happy."

"Hell, Maggie, you are overpaid by about two hundred percent now, plus the greatest perk an office assistant could have, Bull Bullock as your boss. And as far as that remark concerning boyfriends goes, you won't even allow the guys trying to get close to you the time of day. So, enough the smart-ass complaints are concerned, drop it and get your butt back to work." Smiling at the good-natured ribbing she and her long time boss and friend had exchanged, Maggie's reply was short and to the point: "Bull, as in bull crap," and then a pause, "Anything else for now?"

"Nope," Bull snorted, "Call you later, Maggie."

Bull carefully swigged the coffee, knowing from past experience that Maggie's coffee, strong and super-hot, would peel the skin right of your tongue if you didn't enjoy it slowly. So, as he alternately blew and sipped, he picked up the paper and scanned the morning headlines. No earth-shaking events this morning as he turned to page two. Subsequent pages yielded little more of interest, except when it came to the Sports section. Breezing through the first couple of articles about the Texas Rangers pre-season games, the wind up of the Final Four in basketball, and the up-coming playoffs for the Dallas Mavericks.

Bull finally got to the part that perked his interest most of all, his beloved Texas Aggies. The end of spring football practice was on hand and the final Spring Scrimmage game was this coming Saturday. College Station was only about a four-hour drive, and he dang sure was going to be there, come hell or high water.

His wife of twenty years, Melba Lou, was not an Aggie fan, except for trying to keep harmony in the marriage, would probably reluctantly accompany him on this annual pilgrimage. Melba Lou, being a TCU graduate, an archrival of A&M in the old Southwest Conference days, maintained her loyalty to the university in Ft. Worth. In her way of thinking, it made more sense to support the home-town school. Not quite an avid fan as Bull, she nevertheless had converted him over a bit to the TCU Frogs corner, except when game schedules conflicted. On those days, it was no contest with Bull, an Aggie through and through. He was maroon and white all the way.

As he often did when business matters were slow, Bull swiveled his over-stuffed leather office chair to gaze out his large window that, from his second-floor office, overlooked Main Street in downtown Burson. Local employees in downtown businesses headed in both directions exchanging smiles and "Good Mornings" as they scurried to meet opening times. In this small town, population of around eight thousand, most downtown workers knew each other by first name, and being the president of the only bank in town, Bull recognized most of them as they walked past. It was sort of a mental exercise for him each morning to recall their names as they walked past, and something personal about each one. Spouses, children, and where they lived danced through his mind like an old familiar melody of a favorite song. Also, from a business standpoint, it also helped to know something of their financial background. A good memory of those personal details had been a major factor in the long and successful career he had achieved in Banking. Knowing your customers, and establishing a "good old boy" relationship, was essential in this small community. He had honed that skill to perfection.

Chapter Two

The Long-Feared Phone Call

Suddenly, the peaceful silence of the morning was interrupted by a ring of the telephone, line three, his private line. Now who in Hell would be calling me on that line this time of the morning, was his first thought. Swiveling back around to face his desk, he grabbed the phone in his huge left fist, and matter of-fact-like, responded to the caller with a firm: "Bullock here, who is this?"

"It's JJ, Bull, and you ain't gonna like this!"

Bull Bullock did not move from his chair, not even as much as a swivel, for the next several minutes. It was if time was frozen as he gazed out his window, not even noticing the morning pedestrian traffic, that only minutes before had so dominated his attention but now was meaningless to the multitude of scenarios that were endlessly flashing through his mind. "*Damn it, why now?*"

The tenacity of his thought processes was abruptly interrupted as Maggie knocked lightly, and without as much as a pause, entered the room carrying a fresh cup of steaming coffee. "I figured it was about time to perk you up a bit since

I have not heard a peep out of you since that phone call you got about a half-hour ago; must be bad news or something."

"Not really, just a bump in the road," Bull replied. "JJ called with a little problem, some of those guys working on his fence line. Probably needs me to check them out, credit worthy kind of stuff, etc. You know I'll find out what the burr under his saddle is later today. In fact, I'll probably just get all the "Five" together today instead of our usual Friday so I can cut out a little early tomorrow."

Maggie just nodded and after replacing his cup, turned around and headed back to her small reception office just outside of Bull's spacious one. She paused, then asked. "Want me to call the other four, or do you want to handle it personally?"

"Uh . . . I don't have a lot on my desk, so I'll just take care of it. Thanks anyway Maggie."

The other four of the five Burson residents, each an independent owner of their own business, meet for lunch every Friday at the town's most popular restaurant, Gail's Diner. The "Friday Five" was the name originally coined by the owner and manager, Gail Pritchard, who, over the years, had become the proverbial "thorn in their side" because, not only her quick wit but the inquistive interaction with her customers.

Over the span of many years together, The Friday Five had become great friends, mainly because of the weekly meeting at Gail's Diner. In order by seniority within the group: JJ Stevens owner and manager of the Split Aces ranch, Pablo Rodriguez, owner and manager of Pablo's Restaurant, Mal Morris, owner and manager of Rancher's Best Friend Feed Store, and Parker Coburn, owner and manager of Parker Coburn Oil and Gas Company.

Unknown to them now, but the phone call they were about to receive was the one they most feared.

CHAPTER THREE

Burson, A Small West Texas Town

One hundred thirty miles west, and a bit north of Ft. Worth, located in what is most frequently known as West Texas, was Burson, Texas. An average economic situation keeps this small town on a "more or less" even keel, with only slight growth, but at least not losing population as many of like West Texas towns have experienced. The largely Ranch type industry was at the beginning, and still is, the mainstay of the economy. Pick-up trucks, along with one-ton flatbeds with two axles, dual-tires and wheels, have always been the most visual vehicles making up the local traffic. Chevies, Fords, and Dodges are the leading brands and are sold in about equal numbers. Only a few of the increasing popular foreign brands are sighted, but the strong patriotic sentiment of this West Texas area is still to "Buy American."

Secondary to the ranching industry, oil and gas production stills plays an important part in the employment opportunities for the residents. The big oil and gas boom was back in the thirties and at that time, was the primary reason for a huge acceleration of Burson's growth. After the initial good years, and the production of those natural products decreased, the town just settled into a state of "holding on" and for years was just more or less stagnant. Both large and small oil and gas companies began to halt the exploration for new reserves, finding the oil and gas fields to be too expensive to operate and not offsetting the production costs. At least, there was not enough financial gain to satisfy their shareholders. That is when the residents begin to take stock of what was happening and begin to buy up the bargain basement deals the big corporations were offering. Leases were selling for as little as fifteen thousand dollars for a producing well. By doing your own maintenance and with minimal expense from a cleaning rig company, usually a local guy, an old producing well could yield three or four barrels of oil a day, and perhaps a thousand or so cubic feet of natural gas.

With prices in that time at $10 per barrel and $2.50 per thousand cubic feet of gas, an average owner could bring in about $45 to $50 dollars per day for an average producing well. Assuming the normal twenty to twenty-five days of operation per month, and with not too much of the clean out procedure, a little bit of luck thrown in, you could just about return your investment in two or three years. Of course, that meant your personal labor charge was minimal, like free.

At least forty families in Burson have some working interest in a producing oil and gas well. Five small companies have business addresses and occupy self-owned or rental space within the town. All five belong to the Chamber of Commerce and are active in community and civic affairs.

The balance of the business district is like any small Texas town, two major chain clothing stores, JC Penny and Dillard's. Two or three local retail clothing specialty shops are competing with the big boys, just trying to keep their head above water financially. The usual Dairy Queen and McDonald's, and a more recent Sonic drive-in make up the fast-food choices. Local restaurants are somewhat abundant, and business seems to be good, at least adequate, for all of them. American, Chinese, Italian, and Mexican cuisines are all available. A couple of law offices, three real estate brokers, cleaning shops, shoe repair shops, service stations, car dealers, Beauty and barber shops etc. are all profitable, but only just making a living at average income levels.

Two of the more popular hangouts for the residents, Gail's Breakfast Diner and Pablo's Mexican Cuisine Restaurant are prominent in, and essential to, this story.

The most talked about topic in town is the Burson Bobcats. The local high school has about three hundred students in three grades, all tutored by a better than average and very dedicated group of teachers all of whom are widely respected within the town. But scholastics aside, the Burson Bobcats are the pride of every citizen because of their athletic accomplishments. As everyone in Texas knows, High School Football reigns supreme, and is a constant source of pride among Texans. The Bobcats have achieved a great deal of publicity, having won two class 3A state championships within the past three years. Head Coach Jim (Whistler Williams) is in his fourteenth year in that position and has achieved a remarkable 123 to 21 won–lost record. Although widely sought by much larger schools because of his outstanding coaching achievements, Whistler steadfastly declines all offers and loyally stays put in his native home, where he was born and raised.

Basketball never quite gets the publicity or interest that football does in West Texas, but Burson High usually competes well in their district, although it never matches the enthusiasm created by the gridiron boys. Whistler doubles as the assistant coach in basketball to Head Coach Bern Whitlock. Whistler, now fifty-nine years young and with two grown daughters and two near teenage grandsons, is the consummate laid-back granddad. Bern Whitlock, twenty-seven years of age and only in his third season as Head Basketball Coach, and Whistler are near inseparable as co-workers, as well as good friends. Bern and Mary Jo, who before their marriage were High School sweethearts, are expecting their first child in three months. Whistler struts around as if he is the expecting grandpa.

Other sports like many other small schools, baseball, track and field, girls basketball, and tennis were all coached by teachers doing double duty.

A small police force and a sheriff's office with a few deputies complete the definition of a typical small West Texas town, Burson, Texas.

Chapter Four

Five Local Friends Meet for Lunch

It was Thursday, April 24, 1984, at 11:45 a.m. when Parker Coburn hastily removed his jacket and Stetson and flipped them upon the wall rack for coats, etc. on the south wall of Gail's Diner.

"I'd say it's 'bout time you got your ass in gear and got down here. We danged near started without you." Those first words, one many to play out over the next forty-five minutes, came from the very bass, crusty, voice of Phillip Malcolm Morris.

Parker replied curtly: "Don't know why your feathers seemed ruffled, my pal Mal; don't ever remember you being the The Prince of Punctuality."

Bull Bullock sat for a moment displaying little emotion, but then in a soft but demanding voice replied: "Stuff it, Parker, this is some serious crap we got to talk about; and it's way past time for lovey-dovey greetings."

JJ Stephens, dressed in his usual Wrangler jeans, denim western shirt, well-worn Justin boots and sweat lined Stetson

hat just mumbled: "Let's get on it men, I ain't got all day! I got mama cows calving."

The fifth member of this hastily called lunch meeting was Pablo Rodriguez, the owner and full-time manager of Pablo's Mexican Cuisine Restaurant. He chimed in with: " Sí amigos, I no like this waiting and all this suspense. Bull, you called this meeting, what's up?"

"Well, it's like this, gentlemen, we got one big frigging problem on our hands. Chat Cason just woke up, and what's even worse news, he seems to remember things he shouldn't."

Following those two, seemingly simple, sentences from Bull, there was a sustained silence from the other four present at the table.

After about thirty seconds, with no one wanting to be the first to speak, Parker broke the silence: "How did you find out and from whom?"

Bull never got a chance to reply as at that time. Gail Mitchell, owner and do-everything-employee of Gail's Breakfast Diner interrupted: "Parker, got your usual black coffee, straight and hot, just the way you like it. How come you're so dang late holding up the rest of this Friday Five?"

Parker: "Just work, work, work Gail Honey. You, above all people, should appreciate that."

"I'll get back to you young kids a bit later for you order; I got good paying customers to take care of." She wandered off to a table in the corner and continued her good-natured ribbing with another group, a hungry bunch of Mexican fence workers. The northwest corner table at Gail's Diner was the most private table in the establishment. It was by design that Gail had used the quietest part of the restaurant to seat parties up to eight. It was a large round table that could be expanded to seat ten with the insertion of two large table leaves. Bull and the rest of the Friday Five, as they affectionately called their little gathering, met every Friday at 11:30, for "lunch and BS. Although Gail did not take reservations except for large birthday parties, etc. she had reluctantly been persuaded by sweet talk, not to mention good tips, to reserve that table each Friday for Bull's Friday Five. This unusual Thursday meeting perked her curiosity, and she was not going to go through this lunch period without some serious questions being asked.

It was in this, seemingly safe to talk locale, and with Gail out of earshot range, that Bull answered Parker's question. "As you all know, JJ's niece, Martha, works at the John and Betsy Woodson Care Center; and you also know that is where Chat's being cared for the last several years. We've all heard stories 'bout how medical science has never quite figured out why comas occur, why they last as long as they do, and when or why somebody suddenly wakes up from one. JJ's had Martha on notice for a long while to keep an open eye for any signs of Chat's recovery, and she simply did her job. She called JJ about 6:45 this morning, right after arriving for the seven o'clock shift. JJ didn't call me until I got to work; wanted me not to have to answer questions from my Mrs. Curiosity, Melba Lou. You all know that sweet little wife of mine has more curiosity stored up inside her than the Dallas Shelter for Homeless Cats."

Parker, cupping both hands around Gail's coffee, enjoying the aroma as well as the taste, again was the more inquisitive one in the group. "Did Martha know what he said, if anything, and what his prognosis for recovery is, if any?"

Bull: "JJ, why don't you answer that one? You're the one that got it straight from the horse's mouth; I only got second hand knowledge."

JJ paused a moment to make sure that Gail or other patrons were not within earshot, then responded: "Martha did not go into much detail but did say that he was only in the early stage of waking up and struggling to talk. The only remark he made that seems to be relevant to our concerns, is that he asked if had been in a collision. She would monitor Chat's progress and keep me informed."

Pablo was the next of the five to enter the conversation: "Certainly pray for Mr. Cason to recover but I have mixed emotions as to what to pray for."

Mal jumped in, "Count me in as a ditto on that Pablo."

Bull purposely waited a short amount of time before he spoke: 'If no one else has a question or comment, I suggest we end this meeting and keep our ears open to see what happens from here on. Let's keep each other informed."

The Friday Five arose from their chairs and made their way to the check-out counter.

CHAPTER FIVE

Four Years Earlier, the Accident

It was not an unusual time, at 6:30 a.m., for a lot of residents of Burson, Texas, to be on the road toward work, school, or anywhere else, for that matter. However, 5:30 a.m. was not the normal time locals were on their way home. Station KABL, FM radio out of Abilene had just announced the time and Chat Cason took note that, on his way home from work, rather than leaving for work, did seem a little strange. The DJ had just popped on a George Strait tune. Chat was alternately humming and patting the steering wheel, keeping time to the rhythm, while driving along the small county road surrounded by thousands of acres of ranch land. It was early in May 1980, and a slight misty rain, along with a mixture of oil slick build-up from traffic, was just enough to cause the black asphalt pavement to be a bit slick. A further agitation was that the mist was not enough to use the windshield wipers on full speed, but too much to use on the intermediate cycle. Even with this inconvenience, Chat was happy to be near home. After attending a Horse Sale in Houston, it had been a last-minute decision to drive all night and share breakfast with his wife, Joanie, preferring to pass up a night at some small motel with a continental breakfast. Not in his wildest dreams would Chat ever imagine how his life was about to change forever.

Chat Cason, thirty-two years of age, six-foot-two, two hundred eighteen pounds of almost pure muscle, was a rugged handsome West Texas cowboy in every sense of the word. He had excelled in all the major sports, football, baseball, basketball, and even track in a stellar high-school career. Widely sought out by major university recruiters, he had chosen to attend Texas Christian University, and spent four fruitful years pursuing his dream of athletics and ranching.

His athletic career ended on a Saturday afternoon in November of his junior year. As an offensive slot receiver, he was used to taking a pounding each week; and had enjoyed an almost three-year career without significant injury. Leaping high into the air to grab a twenty-eight-yard pass, over the middle from quarterback Bobby Bronson, he was tackled high and low by two safeties from the defensive team. The low tackler caught him just below the knee, buckling it sideways just as he hit the turf, and the second tackler landed hard on top of the already extended leg. Although the hit was hard, it was clean and all within the expected risks of playing Division One football. The ensuing doctor's diagnosis, after extensive x-rays, was not good. That was, sadly, the day that Chat's dream of professional football ended.

Never one to be down and out about anything, Chat put athletics aside and doubled up on his workload in school. He graduated at mid-term the following year and launched full scale into his long-time aspirations to be a horse rancher. With a newly earned degree in ranch management, and with a wealth of contacts from prominent alumni, Chat was on his way to a successful career in ranching.

Shortly after securing a job as the assistant manager for the Double D Quarter Horse Ranch, Chat and his long-time college sweetheart, Joan Elizabeth Atkins, were married in a simple wedding at the Burson United Methodist Church.

After an outstanding performance in his first years as assistant manager, it was obvious to his peers and friends alike that he was a natural in the ranching business. His keen eye for quality horses had resulted in many outstanding awards. Profit from sales had increased to record margins. Four years and two daughters later, Chat assumed the position of general manager of the Double D Ranching Enterprises, Inc., that included cattle ranching as well as quarter horses. Numerous facets of the industry such as breeding, raising livestock, training, sales, shows, etc., were all within the area of his responsibility. At the early age of twenty-seven, Chat was well on his way to the dream life he envisioned since his first summer job on a working Horse Ranch owned by the father of a school friend.

Although he was some ten to fifteen years younger than Bull Bullock and his closest friends, Chat had often joined them for lunch at Gail's Breakfast Diner. It was never by invitation, just a chance meeting that is often the case in small town socials. He had also developed a very cordial relationship with Pablo Rodriguez because of his huge fondness for Tex-Mex food, and Pablo's Mexican Cuisine restaurant being the only restaurant in town specializing in Mexican food.

The other three of the "Friday Five" were also quite well known by Chat. "JJ" Stephens was a fellow rancher, "Mal" Morris a feed store owner, and Parker Coburn, a small oil and gas company owner, all had business interests compatible with Chat's position as general manager for the Double D and often had business dealings with each other. Thus, like in all small towns, each of the central characters was quite familiar with each other, and with their families as well.

The Chevy Silverado Chat was driving was purring along; the engine running sweeter than normal as it always seemed to do with the high humidity of that early misty morning. Little Bob Herring's ranch house was just on his left as he sped by at about sixty miles-per-hour. *Guess Little Bob is having his morning java* about now. Chat had just noticed that the kitchen lights were on in the large, but not pretentious ranch home of the Bob Herring family.

As he approached the almost thirty-degree turn on Hwy 380, and just preceding the small bridge crossing Little Elm Creek, something quite unusual caught his eye. Just east of the bridge and off to his left was the seldom used entrance to the Herring Ranch. It had at one time been the main entrance to original Herring Ranch home.

About ten years earlier, the Senior Bob Herring, like Bob Jr. an only child and whose father had purchased the ranch several years prior to his sudden death with a heart attack, inherited the Herring Ranch and his possessions. After assuming control of the ranch, he and Lillian had remodeled the old house several times before deciding to build the new home. The new home was built about one mile east of the old house, the house Chat had just passed.

What had been two parallel rows of small cedar trees that outlined the gravel driveway was now a group of overgrown and unattended array of dense evergreen foliage. Between two of the trees, and almost hidden from view, a parked vehicle quickly aroused Chat's curiosity. As he turned his head to look back, a shadowy figure moved behind the pickup truck, as if to trying to conceal their presence. "I know that pickup. What the hell is going on here?" he mumbled to himself.

Chat had driven through this curve approaching this bridge at least a few hundred times; but not while driving sixty milesper-hour and looking backwards. No screeching of the brakes occurred, only a sickening sound of metal crashing into a concrete pillar, on the cornerstone of the Little Elm Bridge. The Chevy Silverado crumpled into a maze of twisted metal, broken glass and splintered plastic as it near shattered the formidable concrete opposing force. At that speed, the momentum could not be stopped in place.

The bed of the pickup jerked upward and over the smashed engine compartment and cab. Airborne, the pickup flipped end over front before crashing into the limestone creek bed thirty some odd feet below.

With gasoline and oil leaking everywhere, and steam spewing in all directions, the Chevy finally rolled into a static position, with Chat still buckled inside.

"*Think, damn it, think, what in the hell happened?*" Bleeding profusely from the head and nose, Chat tried in vain to wipe the blood from his eyes. Unable to move his arms, he frantically was crying for answers. Chat was pinned between the dashboard and the rear window, the entire cab crushed into a miniature version of its original size. His head was throbbing as if he had been hit with a sledgehammer, but he felt no pain in his body, only complete numbness.

The seat belt had worked as advertised and had saved Chat's life. Lying in that twisted hunk of metal in a shallow creek bed at 6:05 in the morning, Chat could barely comprehend what was happening to him. *Am I going to die? Does anyone know I'm here? What do I do now? I've got to get help! My God, Joanie, and little Cindi and Carly, what will happen to them?*

Hundreds of similar thoughts raced through his mind as he helplessly lay trapped alone on that fateful April morning. "Pray: Dear God, I have to pray. Our Father, who art in Heaven, Hallowed be . . ." At that moment, Chat Cason drifted into a deep sleep.

CHAPTER SIX

The First 911 Call and The Response

"Help me, please help me!" The broken voice was filled with anguish and constant sobbing, repeated over and over.

The 911 operator replying in a clear steady voice: "Please remain calm and tell me your problem."

"My husband, my husband's been shot," more sobbing, "Hurry, please send help! I think he's dying."

"Your name, please, your name and address?" And with some urgency in her voice, "Please stay calm and speak clearly. We'll send help immediately."

"My name is Betty," voice breaking, "Betty . . . Betty Jean Herring. We live at Herring Road . . . Number One Herring Road, three miles east of town on Hwy 380. Hurry, oh my God, please hurry. I . . . I think he's dying."

"The Bob Herring Ranch, Number One Herring Road, correct?"

"Yes, yes, yes, correct . . . correct, oh my God, please hurry."

The operator tried to instill calm to the situation: "Help is on the way, stay calm and talk to me. Whatever you do, stay on the line. Okay? Are you or anyone in your family in danger? Was it an accident?" And after a long thoughtful pause, "Or did someone shoot him?"

"No, no, it wasn't an accident. Someone shot him. I heard the shot." More uncontrollable sobbing: "I just found him here on the back porch. Oh God, please don't let him die."

The operator with still more urgency and persuasion in her voice: "Did you see the shooter? Are they still there, and are you sure that you and your family are safe?"

"No . . . no, I did not see anyone, and I don't see anyone anywhere. I think the kids are still sleeping upstairs."

Fifteen minutes later, the Burson Police car, no siren but emergency lights flashing, turned right off Hwy 380 and sped down One Herring Road the three to four hundred yards that separated the Herring home from the highway. Only a quarter of a mile behind, the local ambulance was in sight as the Police car screeched to a halt in the concrete pavement of the spacious three car garage attached to the main house.

Officer Phil Dickens bolted from the Dodge Charger and raced to the back of the house and, while galloping, unsnapped the safety strap in the holster that cradled his thirty-eight Smith & Wesson. With one hand caressing the revolver handle, his eyes were searching everything in sight for a possible encounter with what could be a dangerous confrontation. Once he was at the back porch and having momentarily satisfied his own mind that the shooter was no longer in the area, turned his attention to Betty Jean and the victim.

Betty Jean Herring, at least for the time being, was relatively calm. She was seated on the floor, Little Bob's head wrapped in her arms against her breast and was gently patting him on the shoulder.

Blood was oozing from a gaping wound in his chest, and he did not seem to be breathing. Before Officer Dickens could even check Bob's pulse, the paramedics were on the scene and immediately took charge, applying, routine to them, the life saving techniques they were trained to do.

Betty Jean, a petite, attractive woman in her mid-thirties, was clad only in satin, baby blue, pajamas. Barefooted, hands covered in sticky, drying blood, and uncombed blonde locks flowing in the gentle morning breeze, she suddenly panicked.

"Oh God, where are my kids? They must be scared to death. They were asleep when all this happened. I've got to get upstairs."

As soon as she entered the back door, a sudden sense of relief fell over her. Officer Dickens was seated at the kitchen table, with both youngsters, still pajama clad, seated by his side. Milk and cookies were being consumed and it was obvious that the young officer provided comfort to the youngsters, without divulging the real tragedy that had occurred. He would leave that part to their mother. The children's grandparents had been notified and were on their way. Betty Jean was to change into something more appropriate, get whatever she wanted to carry with her, and then he would carry her to the hospital to be with her husband. He further advised her that another officer had arrived on the scene, and was available to help, if needed, with transportation. The grandparents' arrival time was only minutes away, and she would probably have consultation time with them before she left to be with her husband.

Only moments later, Bob Sr. and Lillian Herring arrived at their son's home and after a hurried meeting and tearful exchanges of grief, bundled up their two young grandchildren and loaded them into their Cadillac sedan. Officer Phil Dickens assisted Betty Jean into the patrol car and led the way to the Burson General Hospital. The other officer remained behind to protect the crime scene.

Both cars had hardly turned the corner before Sheriff "Buck" Jones, with two deputies, was approaching One Herring Road. The apparent murder investigation and search for evidence was in progress.

CHAPTER SEVEN

The Second 911 Call

Sheriff Jones, Come in . . . Officer Phil Hawkins here." Thirty seconds later: "Sheriff Jones, Sheriff Jones, Come in . . . This is Officer Phil Hawkins, and this is important."

"This is Buck, Phil. What you got, son?"

"Just passed the Little Elm Bridge on the way with Betty Jean to the hospital; you need to check something."

"Go on!"

"I was so wrapped up in getting to the Herring Ranch on the emergency call, didn't notice on the way to the ranch . . . but just now driving over the bridge, on the north side in the creek, seems to me that there was one heck of an accident. Hard to make out without stopping, and no time for that, but I think it was a totally demolished pickup, smoke still coming up from the vehicle. I'll call 911 but I doubt they got anyone else to send very pronto. Thought you might better check it out."

"Roger, Phil. I got Chuck and Stevie here with me, and Randy is on his way. Soon as he gets here, he and I will go check it out. Don't feel too comfy leaving either Chuck or

Stevie here alone right now. You know, not knowing exactly what happened or who might still be around. Why don't you go ahead and call 911 anyway; maybe they can rouse up someone else to make the trip." There was obvious concern in the Sheriff's voice.

"Roger and out, Buck. Keep me informed." Phil returned the two-way mike to the holder and continued driving as fast as he could safely travel.

Randy pulled into the Herring driveway just a couple of minutes later; Sheriff Jones did not even give him time to exit the car. Grabbing the door handle on the passenger side and lifting his two hundred thirty-two-pound body into the Dodge, he bellowed: "No time to stop here, Randy; it looks like we got another emergency to tend to."

Buck was bringing Randy up to date with what little information he had about the Herring murder, while the young deputy was "pedal to the metal" pushing the Charger to the Little Elm Creek bridge.

With a somewhat subdued voice, after collecting his thoughts, Buck commented: "This has got to be one of those nights when anything that can go wrong, does! Don't have the foggiest idea of what to expect down at that bridge, but from what little info that Phil passed on, I sure as hell don't expect it to be pretty."

Randy replied: "We're gonna know pretty soon, Buck, just about there."

Buck Jones expectations were surely not understated. After parking the sheriff's car near the creek embankment, it became painfully obvious the wreckage they were observing was anything but pretty.

The steep incline down into the creek bottom was an assembly of loose rocks and sandy soil, making their trek downward awkward and difficult, especially so for the overweight sheriff. Randy offered a hand a couple of times, but Buck rebuffed: "Hey, Randy, get your own self down there. I may be old, but I still ain't no pantywaist. Thank you anyhow, but I'll make it on my own."

After a couple of falls and several sliding maneuvers, the two lawmen were approaching the tangled remains of a late model Chevrolet Silverado. It was on its right side in about eighteen inches of rushing water; water that was dancing above and around the smooth river stones reflecting sparkling beams from the early morning light. The younger and much more agile deputy Randy Spears, with athletic grace, easily pulled himself up on the driver side of the pickup, not knowing what to expect when he looked inside. His already racing heartbeat accelerated even more when he looked at the motionless body that was covered in blood, oil, and gasoline. It appeared to be hopelessly lodged between the dashboard, the crumpled steering wheel and the rear cab structure.

With a sharp pitched voice, Randy called out: "Sir, can you hear me? Can you speak to me?" After a short pause, he repeated: "Sir, Sir! If you can hear me, let me know. This is Deputy Sheriff Randy Spears, and I am here to help you. Say something!"

Buck questioned: "Anyone else in there, Randy?"

"Nope, just one male, but he is in one heck of a mess. Better get on the horn and tell whoever they are sending out here better bring some of those jaws of life things; this guy is packed in like he was the extra sardine they tried to crowd in. We're gonna have to cut him out of here for sure."

"Can you tell if he's alive?" Buck asked.

"I can barely reach his neck and he seems to have a light pulse, but he dang sure ain't moving any body parts. Tell them guys they better get a move on; I think he's hanging on by a thread."

Knowing any further attempt to move the body would be futile, Randy lowered himself back into the water below and stated: "While we're waiting on the EMTs, I'll walk over to the impact side and see if anyone else was along that might have been ejected. This guy's seat belt is still fastened. I'm betting if he had someone with him they would have been belted also and still in the cab; as both doors are still intact."

Sheriff Jones, picking his way through the stream back to the embankment that he had earlier descended, acknowledged his approval. "OK, you go check it out. I'm gonna find a dry stone or something to sit on while we wait on the medical boys."

Only a few minutes later, the EMTs arrived on the scene, but it was no longer just another accident happening on a slightly traveled FM road. Autos, Pickups, SUVs, and other assorted modes of transportation were arriving minute by minute. Some came out of curiosity, after the small-town grapevine communication system quickly spread the word, but many were unselfishly offering help.

It was 8:45 a.m. and the slight drizzling rain had subsided. The sun was alternately appearing and disappearing in the mostly cloudy sky, causing shadows to come and go. Scattered applause and prayers could be heard when the EMTs, along with a handful of several hard worker volunteers, managed to pull the almost lifeless body from the twisted steel cage.

While the victim was being strapped into a portable gurney, one EMT was attempting to cleanse the blood from Chat's face to examine the wounds for emergency treatment. Deputy Randy Spears, who had worked tirelessly in helping with the rescue, looked at Chat's face for the first time. His stunned response to the recognition was slow in coming. In a quivering voice: "Oh . . . Oh my God, it's Chat Chat Cason."

During the elapsed time that the emergency personnel were working with the Jaws of Life equipment, Sheriff Buck Jones had managed to climb the embankment and return to the Dodge Charger for a much, needed cup of coffee from the always present thermos bottle. Someone yelled out, repeating Randy's revelation: "Hey, everybody, it's Chat Cason."

Sheriff Jones said to a bystander, "Did I hear what I thought I heard?"

"Yeh," the reply, "Chat Cason; that's what Randy said. I heard it plain as day."

"Damn it, this has to be done right. I got to get to Joanie and the girls, so she hears this in person from me." Almost jump- ing out of the sedan, and in his loudest voice, he yelled to the crowd: "Listen up, you all, this is Sheriff Buck Jones. I'm asking you, out of respect to Chat's wife and family, that no one, and I mean no one, mentions Chat's name 'till I have time to notify her personally. Everybody hear that and I mean not a word . . . Okay? I'm leaving now. It will probably take me about twenty minutes or so, so hold your tongues! Put a lid on it!" He took a short pause and then said, "Randy, get up here quick son; you're going with me."

Chapter Eight

A Long Day at the Hospital

Joanie Cason, having just filled three bowls with steaming oatmeal, three large glasses with orange juice and after retrieving three pieces of whole wheat toast, was preparing to join her two young daughters for their morning breakfast. Cindi, the older at age four and one-half, was a beautiful little blonde with great resemblance to her mother. Carly, blonde as well and three this month, was a little plump for her age. She also possessed a hearty appetite and was by far the more mischievous and animated of the two. Ever the thoughtful mother, Joanie, had just admonished Carly for trying to sneak an extra spoonful of sugar into her oatmeal when she startled by the continuous ringing of the doorbell.

Who could that possibly be at this hour of the morning? In her haste to rise from the table, she upset her own glass of OJ. She quickly ripped a handful of paper towels from the roll on the kitchen counter and placed it over the spill. "Coming," she announced loudly as she hurried to answer the early morning caller. She opened the door to something unexpected.

"Sheriff Jones, what brings you out so early this morning? Is something wrong?"

The Mason County Sheriff was standing unusually erect. His Four Beaver Stetson was rotating from one hand to another as he held it rather awkwardly in front of his rather large mid-section. In a soft, but distinct voice, Sheriff Jones broke the bad news. "Joanie, I hate like all get-out to be the one to tell you this, but Chat has been in an accident . . . You need to come with me to the hospital. Now."

"No," she replied as her voice begin to tremble. "What, How . . . is he hurt bad? Tell me, is he hurt bad? What happened, was it a wreck or what?"

"Joanie, we don't know much of the details yet; he is alive . . . but pretty badly hurt. The ambulance is on its way to the hospital; and should be getting there just about now. Grab whatever you need, and I'll rush you there. Randy will take good care of the girls and bring them down later; or you can decide what you want to do with them after you know more about his condition. You know, like who you want to sit with them and so forth. You might want to find out more about what's going on before you have them brought down to the hospital. Anyway, that's your call."

Not a second was wasted as Joanie grabbed her purse and a light jacket, hugged her kids, and assured them both with: "Mommy has got to go away for a little while, but I'll be back soon. Officer Randy is going to help you finish breakfast and play with you 'till I get home. Please be good for the nice man." Trying hard to contain her composure in front of her children, she bolted from the door and into the already idling car of Sheriff Jones.

Less than twenty minutes later, Buck and Joanie wheeled into the portico for the emergency room at Burson General

Hospital. Only small talk had ensued between them in their rush to the hospital. Most of the conversation centered around Buck's attempt to comfort her with words of encouragement and hope. Joanie, for the most part, held up reasonably well emotionally, considering the devastating news she had just received.

Buck was letting his thoughts wander: *She's strong . . . she's a keeper. Chat got a dang good one when he got her!*

The EMT guys met Buck and Joanie as they entered the ER. "He's stable, Mrs. Cason; a couple of Doctors are with him as we speak. Took a real nasty lick to the head, broken ribs, and a lot of cuts and bruising, but the seat belt pretty-well prevented any great damage to the rest of his body. Course, that's our assessment; the Docs will do a full work up on him and get the full picture of his condition. It will probably take a while to do all the tests, but I'm sure they'll get you back there as soon as possible. They're aware that you were on your way here and, as soon as we sighted you, we relayed that info."

"I would really like to see him as soon as possible. Can I see him before they do the tests?" Joanie asked.

"I'm sure that they want you back there as soon as possible also. But right now, Chat's condition is their main priority. I don't think a distraction is what they need right now."

Buck Jones, like a gentle giant, moved closer and wrapped his arms around her as she began to sob uncontrollably. He then ushered her to a nearby lounge and sat beside her, tightly squeezing her hand, providing the security she so desperately needed at this hour.

Although in Joanie's mind hours had passed, but only approximately forty minutes had elapsed from the time she and Buck had entered the ER.

How much longer, Dear Lord, How much longer? Is he critical? Oh . . . Lord . . . Jesus . . . please let him be okay. What's taking so long? They should have notified me of something by now.

Approximately three more gut-wrenching hours had passed when Buck alerted Joanie: "The doctor's coming."

Two automatically operated doors, separating the visitors lounge from the ER patient rooms, swung apart as Dr. Jonas Mehaffey strode briskly into the waiting room area. Still clad in the traditional green scrubs, mask lowered to his neck, and prematurely grey hair protruding from the elastic bound head covering, the surgeon commanded presence. Joanie, as well as practically everyone in the county, personally knew the respected surgeon approaching her. His reputation as a surgeon and as a person was impressive and untainted. Speechless at that moment, Joanie just waited for the doctor to speak.

"Good news and some bad news, Joanie! Chat is conscious, and that is good; but on the other side of the coin, there are some potentially bad problems that we are going to have to hope and pray don't mess up the recovery. General body condition, only a couple of broken ribs and a fractured left fibula, is not serious. The primary area of concern is the head injury. He suffered a severe injury to the head, and blood has accumulated on the left side of the brain. We did some intricate surgery and think that we have the bleeding under control. However, keeping the swelling down and preventing the pressure on his brain from building is both the worry and the unknown factor. We're reasonably confident that we have it under control, but only time will tell. I don't want to unnecessarily alarm you, but I don't want to sugar coat it either. Prayer is the best thing we got going for us right now."

Joanie's voice was trembling: "Thank you Lord, thank you . . . and thank you Dr. Jonas, you'll never know how much . . . When can I see him?"

"Now, but only for a few minutes; he's slipping in and out of consciousness and will probably continue that for a few days. I'll take you back there now if you're ready."

She grabbed her purse and was accompanying Dr. Jonas to Chat's room. But after only three or four steps, she wheeled around and hugged the sheriff who had not, for a single minute, left her side.

"Thank you for what you did for me, Buck. I'll never forget it! NEVER!" Joanie said.

"I'm really glad I could be there for you, Joanie. Anytime! Tell Chat we are all pulling for him."

"Will do!" she replied.

The automatic swinging doors worked on cue.

Back at the Parker home, Randy Spears had fulfilled his "Mr. Mom" role to perfection. Alternately keeping Cindi and Carly entertained with a multiple number of games that a three- or four-year-old would enjoy, plus responding to the constant repetition of phone call inquiries, he began to think that his proverbial "cup had run over."

"Guess I'm not too bad at this Mr. Mom stuff after all," he softly spoke to himself. One of the many phone conversations, between he and Parker, friends and neighbors, had resulted in a temporary fix to his Mr. Mom problem. Coach "Whistler" Williams and his wife, Mary Jo, had been long-time friends of Chat and Joanie. Having grandkids of their own, both had insisted on coming over to the Parker home and taking charge as grandparents in chief. Also, several times in the past, they had substituted as Cindi and Carly's grandparents when Chat and Joanie were unable to find a sitter. Both girls were comfortable with the stand-in Papa and Mama. "Whistler" and Mary Jo's reputation, outstanding as it was, made it a "no brainer" decision for Randy to relinquish his duties as sitter and homemaker. After a couple of hugs from the Parker girls, who did not want their newly found friend to leave, Randy excused himself and waved goodbye. A clerk, from the Sheriff's office, had arrived with transportation back to the office.

Dr. Meheffey, tossing his surgical bonnet into the spoiled clothes bin as they entered, assisted Joanie into the CCU room on the second floor of Burson General Hospital. The room, rather large, was divided into six bed-units. All were surrounded by winter-green colored curtains attached to a circular track; designed for efficiency and often-needed privacy. Each unit was equipped with the latest in digital medical accessories. A special election three years ago, offering a bond authorization to update the hospital, had been approved by the county electorate. The favorable vote had been overwhelming. The renovation project had just been completed two months ago. It was Chat's good fortune that the allure of state-of-the-art medical equipment in a ultra-modern hospital had the added advantage of attracting two new outstanding surgeons to the community, one being Dr. Jonas Meheffey.

With a comforting arm around Joanie's waist, Dr. Jonas directed her into unit number three. He quietly closed the curtains around her and politely requested: "Just a few minutes, Joanie. I'll leave you two alone for a bit. Please . . . don't force him to talk. Just knowing that you are here will do him a world of good." He parted the curtains and walked away.

Except for the heavy layers of bandage around his head and the usual array of tubes and wires connected to almost endless parts of his body, Chat looked much better than Joanie expected. She carefully lifted his hand, taped blood pressure hose and IV attached, and lovingly placed it into both of hers. To her surprise and great relief, Chat slowly opened his swollen black eyes and turned his head toward his beautiful wife. In a barely audible voice: "Hi Honey Bun! Guess I don't look too pretty."

Weeping crocodile sized tears, and smiling at the same time, she joyfully replied: "Well, you might not win any handsome hunk contests right now, but you'd still get my vote."

"Can't figure out what happened, Hon, it all is kind of . . . fuzzy, you know."

"Dr. Jonas gave me strict orders. You are not to talk, you understand? Just rest, and I'll be right here beside you. I am not leaving you."

"But the girls, where are the girls? Are they okay?" "They're in good hands, Whistler and Mary Jo have them. I talked to them both just before coming in to see you. Now, stop chattering and do what the Doctor said, rest!!"

Chat reluctantly closed his eyes; and almost immediately drifted off into dream world. It would be a long restless day and night for both the patient and the visitor.

Chapter Nine

The Futile Attempt to Save a Life

Earlier that morning, and in the same emergency room where later in the day Chat Cason was fighting for his life, James Robert Herring Jr. lost his battle to survive. Dr. Clifton Conner turned to the two nurses and one intern, took a long look at the wall clock, and solemnly pronounced: "I'm calling it at seven forty-two. I'll break it to Mrs. Herring. Thank all of you for your effort. We did all we possibly could do."

While turning to leave the room to meet Betty Jean Herring, attempting to condition himself for the proper words to say, he abruptly stopped and added: "Although it's meaningless, even with that gaping hole through his chest, the law requires an autopsy. I'm sure that you already knew that. Just doing my job."

Obvious sadness filled the room. No one, regardless of how many times you have worked a similar traumatic experience, ever gets used to losing the battle to save a patient's life. The intern was directed to notify the county coroner.

Dr. Conner made the obligatory visit to the waiting room and the meeting with Burson's newest widow. Betty Jean, with family and friends gathered in a crowed circle around the news bearer, listened intently as the details unfolded. The cause of death was, as already acknowledged, a gunshot wound through the chest. It had burst the upper aorta valve and death had been almost instantaneous. Thankfully, he had not suffered. The doctor and his team had worked in vain and had spared nothing in their attempts to save him. The injury was just too devastating to overcome. The time lapse in getting to the hospital was not a factor. He additionally made them aware of the impending autopsy.

With sincere compassion, he attempted to answer the deluge of questions that followed. Betty Jean, already knowing within her heart it was next to impossible that he was alive, remained remarkably calm. Of all the family, she asked the fewest number of questions. With the usual regrets and offers of further help in any way possible, Dr. Conner took his leave.

The assembled family members and friends, after milling about for a few minutes, slowly and tearfully departed the hospital. More friends and family had hastily gathered and were waiting at the Bob Herring Sr. home, for their impending arrival. Now One Herring Road was now a crime scene and returning there, at this time, was not an option.

CHAPTER TEN

The Initial Meeting of the Murder Investigation

Shortly after leaving Joanie Parker at the hospital, Sheriff Buck Jones returned to his office adjacent to the county jail at the corner of Fifth and Owens St. His first order of business was to phone Chief of Police Ward Thompson. "Ward, Buck here; need to meet you, like post haste." "Affirmative, Buck," Ward said, "your place or mine?"

"Your call," Buck said, "makes me no difference."

"I can be there in ten."

"That works for me; bring it on." "I'm on my way!"

Both officers of the law cradled their phones.

Buck Jones had not let his compassion for Joanie interfere with his duty to do his job. While he and Randy had been driving to the Parker house earlier that morning, he was diligently working the two-way radio with the two deputies that he had earlier dispatched to the Herring Ranch. He was ordering a thorough search of the grounds surrounding the murder scene. His advice was that: "No piece of possible evidence should be overlooked, no matter how insignificant it appeared." Officer Phil Hawkins, the first law person on the scene, had secured the grounds adjacent to the home with the familiar yellow *Crime Scene Investigation: Do Not Enter* tape. Other police officers were still on the premises.

Ward Thompson knocked lightly on the open door to Buck's office: "Okay now?"

"Grab a seat, Ward. Nice to see you, but I wish it was under different circumstances."

The Sheriff rose from his chair and the two lawmen exchanged a firm handshake. Ward pulled up a chair, placed his hat on Buck's desk, and leaned forward as he spoke: "Looks like we got a real *hot potato* this time. What you thinking?"

"Well, I suppose if we get real technical, my office has jurisdiction on this one; seeing as how that Herring House sits just outside of the city limits. However," and he paused to gather his thoughts, "the property in that spacious front yard is more than likely within the city. You'd have to have a survey to ascertain that, but I personally don't think anyone cares one way or the other."

"I'll buy that . . . so what are you suggesting?"

The Sheriff leaned back in his swivel chair: "I kinda think, this being such a high-profile case because of it being who it was, we might want to join forces on this one and pool our resources. One thing I am sure of: we need to get on top of this real quick-like."

Ward sighed and replied: "No argument with me on that. Let's do it!"

"Okay, it's a go! I'll see what my boys come up with, and you do the same with yours. Let's get back together; no later than a couple of days."

"Good for me! Meanwhile, got any ideas regarding suspects?"

"Nope, other just mind rumbling about all the folks that ain't gonna be shedding any tears about his sudden demise," Buck said.

"Ditto on that. But I can't help feeling really bad for Betty Jean and the little ones; really going to be tough on them."

"Yeah, but you know Ward, as many times as my boys have been called to that house by Betty Jean reporting spousal abuse when Little Bob had been drinking, wouldn't be totally surprised that she might be involved; not the trigger puller, but somehow connected."

"Well, that's food for thought. But as much as she loves those little girls, I think that pretty well rules her out."

"Pretty sure you're right on that call. But I'll tell you one thing, if he ever does anything to harm those little girls, I'll throw his butt so far back in jail where it's so dark he'll beg for a flashlight just to see the potty."

"Ditto on that also, Buck."

Leaning back in his chair with hands folded behind his head, Sheriff Jones: "Ahh . . . just thinking out loud, I'm suspecting that's 'bout all of the crime solving my old brain can handle for now. I'll rest it for a while and let my boys do the work for a bit. I'll stay in close touch with you."

"Good enough, see you later." The chief grabbed his hat, rose from his chair, nodded, and left the office.

CHAPTER ELEVEN

Robert Wilson Bullock

Robert Wilson Bullock, born and bred Texan, honor graduate of Texas A & M class of 1958, came to Burson as an ambitious young newcomer following an in-school interview for an opening in the new West Texas First National Bank. The only bank in town, recently purchased by group of investors from Abilene, were looking for young intelligent personnel to replace the aging current president, who was eager to retire.

Finishing fourth in his graduating business class, and having four straight summers of working in the Bryan First National Bank near College Station, made young Bob Bullock an attractive prospect for the position of assistant manager. Retiring president Charles Gray had agreed to remain active in his position for one year to train his replacement, and to continue as a paid advisor for the following year. Only two other prospects were invited to personal interviews, and after a few days of anxiety, Bob was invited to a second interview, at which two of the major stockholders were present. It turned out to be no contest as young Robert Wilson was formerly offered the position. Charles Gray and the two stockholders were more than impressed with the young man's knowledge of the business aspect of banking and his engaging personality. His leadership potential was obvious, and the young man did not disappoint. Only eleven months after arriving in person, and with a strong endorsement from his mentor retiree Charles Gray, Robert Wilson Bullock was promoted to the position of president of the Burson First State Bank, with a starting salary and bank stock that far exceeded his expectations.

Exactly two years after his initial employment in Burson, Bob married the only true love of his life, Melba Lou Evans, at an outdoor summer wedding at the beautiful botanic gardens in her hometown of Fort Worth, Texas. Sweethearts from the first meeting at a tailgate party at a TCU versus Texas A&M football game, it was only a matter of waiting for the proper time to tie the traditional matrimonial knot. Bob's promotion provided the financial security he had promised himself that he would provide for her and hopefully, later, young Bullock children. Sadly, after two or three years and many medical examinations, it was determined that Melba Lou was unable to conceive. After fighting off bitter disappointment, Melba Lou thrust herself and her energies into civic and volunteer work for her church and numerous local charities. Because of their set-back in plans for a traditional family, Bob, and Melba Lou's love for each other was only strengthened during the following years, as they solely relied on each other in times of need. As the years went by, Bob and Melba Lou became one of the most loved and respected couples in this small West Texas community.

As a young man, Bob Bullock grew up in the small town of Hawley, twelve miles north of Abilene. His father was a manager of a major home improvement store in Abilene and commuted back and forth to their home in Hawley, Bob's mother was a math teacher in the local high school. An honor student throughout his entire high school career, Bob won many awards including that of the outstanding student in his senior year.

Tall for his age, he was an outstanding basketball player for Hawley High but never had interest in any of the other sports, but instead concentrated on his studies, particularly in math. Bob did have one other natural talent, and that was largely because of his mother's insistence that he take piano lessons. After first being negative about the idea of playing piano, the more he practiced, the more enthusiastic he became about his new talent. After his second year of lessons, he developed the habit of what is called a "good ear" for music, and could play almost anything you could sing or hum without reading printed music.

Although young Bullock never lacked from having dates with young Hawley girls, he became even more appealing and was often asked to play their favorite songs during the lunch hour on the cafeteria piano. Usually, there would be as many as seven or eight young ladies surrounding the piano and singing along.

It goes without saying that young Bob Bullock had an outstanding high school experience.

Chapter Twelve

Margaret Ann Burke

Margaret Ann Burke, five-foot-five, and one-hundred-thirty-five evenly distributed pounds, was a striking forty-one-year-old single. She had become an irreplaceable key employee in her first and only full-time job. She wore her light brown hair medium to short length, depending on the season or whatever persuasion her long-time hairdresser exerted over her on her appointment day. At the age that most people in her profession required glasses for the exhaustive amount of fine print reading and typing required, she still maintained 20/20 vision, and often good naturally kidded Bull about her superior eyesight. Bull, on the other hand, only required reading glasses of which he kept at least eight to ten pair scattered around various parts of his office and the building proper. She always wore tasteful clothing, nothing flashy or revealing, but perfectly correct for the position she held.

Maggie was extremely respected by other employees and her peers, having been elected five different times as president of the Burson Secretaries Club and was twice voted employee of the month, an award given annually by the Chamber of Commerce.

Most of her friends, who loved and respected her so much, knew little about her other than her past twenty-four years in Burson. Among those with whom she was acquainted, it was quite well known that she was very private about her years prior to moving to this small West Texas town. Most of her friends had just given up on inquiring about her past and accepted her for being the wonderful individual that she was at this time. However, one person did know of her past, the whole story, and never revealed or talked of it to no-one, absolutely no-one, Bob Bullock.

Having read an ad in the classified help wanted section of the Wichita Falls Express, Margaret Ann Burke entered the Burson First National Bank promptly at opening time of 9:00 a.m., only two months after Robert Wilson Bullock had been named president of the same. The ad had mentioned that a secretary and typist with some bookkeeping knowledge was needed. It also stated that a recent graduate with superior grades and personality would be considered even with no prior experience. The position offered a reasonable salary with limited benefits, but future raises and extended benefits would be added with tenure. Mrs. Smedley, a cashier temporarily filling in as Mr. Bullock's Secretary, greeted Margaret at her downstairs desk and offered her an application form to fill out. After completing the form and double checking it for accuracy, she returned the form and was asked to wait in the lobby while the application was reviewed before a personal interview was scheduled. She was offered and accepted a cup of coffee and anxiously awaited the next step.

Fifteen minutes turned into thirty, and then into forty, as Margaret nervously awaited some word, but no word or interaction was forthcoming. And suddenly, a very tall and quite attractive young man appeared from one of the side doors and strode briskly toward her.

Extending his hand as he approached and in a not loud, but forceful voice, "Miss Burke; may I call you Margaret?" and without pausing for an answer, "I'm Robert Bullock, Welcome." Margaret leaped to her feet and extended her hand in response and firmly returned the handshake.

"Thank you so much for seeing me personally Mr. Bullock. I was not expecting to see you. I was anticipating an interview with Mrs. Smedley."

"Actually Ruthie, Mrs. Smedley's first name, is one of our senior cashiers and just pitching in to help me the last couple of months until we could get a little better organized. She is knowledgeable about our business and has been a great help to me during my transition period. But now, she needs to get back to cashiering and I need a secretary. Hence the ad in the Express, and now here you are. So, please follow me to my office and let you and I get acquainted."

Burson First National Bank's new young executive, politely led Margaret up the generously wide stairway to his office while offering small talk about the weather and such. Only pausing momentarily and with a hand gesture, he invited her to enter his spacious office and to be seated in one of the two elegant leather covered chairs immediately in front of his desk.

"Before we get started, may I get you a glass of water or soda out of the snack room next door?" Robert inquired.

"Thank you so much, but no. Mrs. Smedley brought me a generous cup of delicious coffee and I'm fine for now." Margaret sat erect on the front edge of her chair, knees together and both feet squarely on the floor. Robert Bullard seated and leaning forward, hands cradling her application, was confirming the impression of one who was anxious to listen to Miss Burke state her qualifications for the open position of secretary to the president.

He spoke first: "I have read and reread your application, Miss Burke. Your grades in school were outstanding, and the letter of recommendation from Dean Johnson was impressive. However, I was intrigued about his remarks regarding your dedication to your schoolwork, and your inner drive to excel despite the hardship you endured in your childhood. He alluded to the fact that you were an orphan and spent most of your life in an orphan's home. Also, he mentioned that you have overcome tremendous hardship during your business school enrollment. Would you care to explain?"

Margaret squirmed nervously in her chair and waited several moments before answering. As she hesitated, pondering her response, to what to her was a subject too difficult to discuss, tears begin to slightly fill her eyes. Reaching quickly for a tissue from the ever-present box on his desk, Robert handed it to her explaining: "I'm so sorry. I did not mean to put you in an uncomfortable position."

After regaining her composure and a few moments when neither spoke, Margaret decided to go for broke. She desperately needed this job and complete honesty was probably the best course of action. In the few minutes she and Mr. Bullock had been together, she had sized him up and, considering herself a good judge of character, decided he was someone she could trust to keep her secret. "I also, am sorry." She paused again, momentarily dabbing her eyes with the tissue. "It is part of my life that I have kept secret, but I feel I can trust you. And I know you need complete honesty from me, and I desperately need this job, so, I will tell you everything about myself."

The next twenty some odd minutes was a complete explanation of her life in a nutshell. With only vague memories of her parents, both killed in a murder/suicide, she had spent her entire childhood in an orphanage. Her delegated parents in the home were nice and loving to her, but as she grew older, she became resentful that she could not have parents and siblings like "normal" kids that she knew outside the home. Looking back on that time of her life, she realized that her ambition to succeed in life was only intensified by her upbringing without a normal childhood and normal parents. That explained the first part of his question and now for the hard part, his question regarding the hardship she endured in business school.

"Mr. Bullock, may I take you up that glass of water you offered before I finish?" she asked.

"Gladly," he replied. "Back in a jiff." Only moments later he returned carrying two sparkling glasses of ice water. "Hope that you enjoy well water. Water is so scarce around here that we have been buying water from one of my client's wells for drinking. Took a little getting used to the taste, but now that I have gotten used to it, I like it much better than our city water."

Waiting an appropriate amount of time, he quietly spoke again. "Take your time please. We are in no rush."

In a more subdued voice, Margaret painstakingly revealed the secret she had confided in only one person previously, Dean Johnson. Regretfully, she told of a one-night romantic encounter that had left her pregnant. The father, a young teenager like she herself, refused to acknowledge to his parents what had happened and had begged her to have an abortion.

Having been reared in an orphanage with strong Christian ties, to her, that was not an option. With Dean Johnson's help, a family was located that would assume the financial responsibilities for the prenatal care and childbirth. Legal papers were signed prohibiting all claims of parenthood or visits or communication with the child forever. Knowing that the child would have the home and parents she never had, she reluctantly agreed to the terms, but with one stipulation. She insisted on meeting the parents in their home to have the assurance that her child would be raised in a good Christian home with loving parents. That condition was agreed to and shortly afterwards a meeting in the home of the prospective adoptive parents was arranged. After visiting with the couple, soon be new parents, and a brief questioning session, she was satisfied that the criteria that she had insisted for her soon to be born baby more than met her expectations. The legal contract binding both parties was notarized the following day. Six months later, in Abilene Memorial Hospital Maternity Ward, she saw her beautiful baby girl for the first time, but only for a few minutes. Though tears filled her eyes, she had known hardship and disappointment much of her life, and once again it was time to suck it up and get on with her life. God had given her another chance and she was determined to make the most of it.

All contact with the baby's father had concluded after her refusal to consent to an abortion, and her interest in dating was next to nothing due to her heartbreaking previous experience. Although she would not rule out ever dating again, and a few times she had been tempted, she was intent on locating a job, having a nice apartment in a small town with no big city or social pressures. In other words, just be a hard-working gal leading a normal life, something she had never experienced in her lifetime.

Young Robert Bullock had not spoken a word during the almost one hour he had intently listened to her almost unbelievable tale of woe. Having grown up with two loving parents in an above average income climate, he almost had to reach for a tissue for himself as his eyes were beginning to moist as her story unfolded. Again, no words were spoken for a few minutes as he collected his thoughts. Margaret, exhausted, but relieved to have gotten it all off her chest, sat quietly and motionless.

Bob Bullock cleared his throat and softly said: "First of all Margaret, as God is my witness, your secret is safe with me. I have two more interviews of which I am obligated, one later today and one tomorrow. I am tempted to hire you on the spot, but I do not take appointments lightly and it would be unprofessional if I did not give the applicants the courtesy of an interview. I will call you tomorrow and let you know my decision. I also do not want to embarrass you, but do you have money for dinner, and do you have a place to stay tonight?"

"The answer is yes to both. Dean Johnson was kind enough to lend me some advance funds to take care of me during my job search. He provided enough to see me through my first paycheck, provided," she chuckled, "it doesn't take too long to find a job."

Rising from his chair and extending his hand: "Great, l look forward to calling you tomorrow. If it all works out as I am expecting, we can get together again tomorrow afternoon and go over the money and benefit things. Oh, do you have a phone number where you are staying?"

"l do, It's the Baker Inn, just up the street," she said. "Great. I know the owners, clients of mine, nice place.

Please forgive me, I have a call waiting and I think it's a business client I've been expecting. I'll have Mrs. Smedley show you out. Just leave your room phone number with her. Have a nice day, Margaret. It's been a pleasure meeting you."

CHAPTER THIRTEEN

Parker Coburn Forms His Own Company

Parker, all five-foot-ten and equally distributed one-hundred-seventy-eight pounds of him, was an easy going, laid-back young entrepreneur that truly loved his job and his small company. He was fiercely loyal and generous to his small fulltime staff of office employees, as well as with his approximately twelve contract employees. The number of contract employees constantly changed according to needs of the time. And because of his unquestioned honesty and straightforward approach to business practices, he had rightfully earned the trust and respect of all with whom he had business dealings.

Ten years earlier, and after two years of junior college followed by eight years of work in the oil fields in around Odessa and Midland, Texas, Parker's career was at a turning point. At one stage or another in his career, he had mastered almost every job associated with oil exploration. From roustabout to chief driller, he was an eager student of the occupation and worked long and hard to succeed. His diligence, rewarded by his taking advantage of the extraordinary amount of overtime hours available, had resulted in the accumulation of a lot of money of which he religiously saved; and with personal pleasure sacrifices, guarded with great discipline.

On a cold, rainy morning in January of 1970, Parker Coburn approached Margaret's desk.

Ann Jones, the personal secretary of Bob Bullock, president and chief financial officer of the Burson National Bank. The attractive lady, seated in her office chair and furiously typing, swiveled her chair from the small typewriter desk to her left, greeted the potential client with a cherry: "Good morning Sir; and may I help you?"

"Yes, Ma'am; and good morning to you also." With a bit of apprehension creeping into his voice, he continued, "Would it, uh, be possible to see Mr. Bullock, please?"

"I would be happy to check with Mr. Bullock for you," Margaret said. "May I please have your name and the nature of your business?"

"Parker Coburn" was the reply, "and it's regarding a loan, Ma'am, a business loan."

Margaret motioned to a nearby sofa. "Please have a seat. I'll notify Mr. Bullock that you are waiting."

As she arose from her chair and briskly headed into the adjoining office, Parker could not help but notice the well endowed and almost picture-perfect developed body of the one Margaret Ann Jones. Musing to himself: *Must be around thirty or so, but that is one nice looking gal. If this deal goes through, I'm going to be looking for a secretary just like her.*

There was little time for further fantasizing moments as the well-stacked secretary returned shortly and offered the invitation: "Mr. Bullock will be pleased to see you. Please follow me."

Bob Bullock, thirty-three years of age, with thinning brown hair prematurely graying in the temples, carried his two-hundred-thirty pounds on six-foot-two frame that created a larger-than-life presence. The tailored blue pinstripe suit and freshly shined alligator loafers affirmed his obvious executive and financial status. Already to his feet, he walked around his massive mahogany desk, extended a huge right hand and offered the greeting: "Mister Coburn, nice to meet you, please have a seat."

"Nice to meet you also, Mr. Bullock and thank you." Bob Bullock took a seat in the nearest of the two chairs directly in front of the President's desk, pulled it slightly forward, and leaned back against the plush soft leather back, attempting to relax.

Bob Bullock initiated the conversation: "Maggie, no one around here calls her Margaret, told me that you are interested in a business loan; like to fill me in on the details? You know, for instance, what kind of business, where will it be, and how much money do you need etc.?"

Parker leaned forward and with growing confidence, offered his justification for the requested loan. With forty thousand dollars of his personal five-year savings as a show of good faith, and a frank discussion of his experience and knowledge of the oil exploration industry, Parker Coburn emerged from Bob Bullock's office some two hours later having secured a one hundred-thousand-dollar line of credit. Liens on future equipment and facilities would be required and forthcoming. It goes without saying that the experienced bank president, having spent several years as chief loan officer before ascending to the position he presently occupied, was duly impressed. It also marked the beginning of a long-time personal relationship between the young banker and the owner of the newest business in town; Coburn Oil & Gas Company, Burson, Texas, USA.

The first order of business for Parker was to locate and purchase an office building, and that happened on only the third day of canvassing the small city for available property. Located just west of the beginning of downtown, and unoccupied, was the former Hi Ho restaurant. The actual building, approximately fifty feet off the highway, had ample room for parking in front. The total lot was close to one and one-half acres in size; quite enough space to fence and park future company trucks and equipment. The spacious former dining area could be easily remodeled by dividing walls and convert the one-time diner into four separate offices and an extra-large reception area. The kitchen would be reduced in size and maintained as a small dining area for the staff, and the remaining part of the kitchen converted into a miscellaneous storage area.

His vision near completed, Parker set out for the task of actual construction. No architect required here, just hand-drawn plans on grid sheets by Parker himself sufficed. A recommendation from Bob Bullock had resulted in a construction contract with an elderly, semi-retired, home builder. Along with his son and three contract workers, Sam Patterson completed the project in less than six weeks.

The final touch, a small but elegant sign bearing the new company's name and logo, was added above the front door. Late into the evening of that day of completion, and as the sun accelerated its descent into a cloudless western sky, Parker stood alone by his pickup in the front lot. The pride of accomplishment filled his heart and mind; and was revealed by the slight smile on his tanned face.

Step one down, so much for that! He continued his thoughts: *Now for step two, a competent quality staff. That starts tomorrow.*

CHAPTER FOURTEEN

Parker Coburn Hires Staff for His Company

Much of Parker's previous six weeks had been as a hands-on advisor for the office remodeling project, constantly recommending changes, or personally purchasing office furniture and equipment. But as busy as he was, he still managed to answer requests for employment opportunities in reply to classified advertising he had placed in nearby city newspapers. Personal interviews were already scheduled for the following Monday.

The most important position, that of geologist, was pretty much already settled. Paul Hicks, who had worked with Parker with his previous employer, and was a close friend, had agreed to join the fledgling company. The only holdup was the time involved in giving proper notification of his resignation and the relocation of his family to Burson.

Only the remaining office positions were scheduled for interviews. Contract employees would be added as required.

Monday arrived and so did Parker Coburn, his first day on the job in his own personal office. A small group of hopefuls entered and departed his office as he dutifully screened a variety

of young and old alike for the four remaining positions, one of which was that of his personal secretary. The last interview of the day was no other than Mary Marilyn Martin, not overly attractive but very personal and someone that he occasionally dated recently in Midland. Being cautious, and after expressing his concern that he was not too anxious to mix business and pleasure, Parker had promised he would give her application serious consideration. In an apologetic manner, he explained he still was obligated to do previously scheduled interviews and would personally inform her of his decision within a couple of days. But in his own mind and not stated verbally, it would be after sleeping on it.

And after sleeping on it, and even before the impending interview with another want-to-be applicant, Parker decided Marilyn would be his first personal secretary. Besides, he continued to convince himself: She wasn't a bad looker, tons of personality, easy going and without knowing for sure, probably a great sex partner. Even marriage was not out of the realm of possibility, as he had permitted himself to dream of sharing his new entrepreneurial career with a loving and caring spouse. Who knows? This might be the one! The few previous dates they had shared were enjoyable and although not altogether that romantic, the easy feeling of compatibility was a definite asset. He had, for sure, felt a romantic connection, but did not feel at ease in pursuing it. He spoke loudly to no one in particular: "Yep, who knows? This . . . just . . . might . . . be . . . the one."

Mary Marilyn reported for work early the following Monday morning. Three of four, the remaining staff of new hires, would report with two weeks. Paul Hicks, having secured a good faith early release, would be on hand by the middle of next week. The bulk of work, in the beginning, would fall to Parker and Marilyn, and a lot of work was there for the doing. The design of office forms, along with letter and office stationary, organizational duties with job descriptions, payroll procedures etc., all required long and frustrating hours on the job. Nine-to-Five, was just a myth, and by no means a reality.

No one, not even the optimistic, hard-working owner, could have predicted the immediate success of the new company. Sales were booming and expansion was much quicker than expected. An increased line of credit was an easy sell to Parker's friend and banker. The office staff worked amazingly well together and efficiently as a team. Parker and Marilyn were always there to set the example for hard work and commitment, and quick to give praise and credit to the other staffers.

Chapter Fifteen

Parker's First House and Possible Romance

Almost six months to the day after opening, Parker purchased a three-bedroom house only a few blocks from his office. Bob Bullock had initiated the contact from one of his clients, the Hailey family, who were transferring to a new job in his hometown of Abilene. Having spent most of his adult life moving from one job location to another, Parker had not lived in anything other than a small apartment and had never purchased any house furnishings except electric appliances, televisions, radios, etc. After near six weeks of closing, Parker found himself in need of a complete array of new furniture, and particularly needing a woman's taste for that sort of decorating expertise. Marilyn was more than happy to help with the selection, so the following days after work became extensive shopping hours for the boss and his right-hand employee.

One late Thursday night, after several attempts to determine the proper place to locate the newest furniture delivery, a huge, overstuffed leather couch, they both reclined in complete exhaustion on the couch, feet propped up on

the coffee table, neither saying a word, just totally relaxing. Both had removed their shoes and neither spoke for several minutes.

Marilyn, breaking the silence of the evening: "I think we made a pretty damn good team, Boss."

Not getting a response from Parker, and thinking that he had dozed off, she playfully placed her bare feet upon his sock-clad feet and pushed them off the table. With no expression of annoyance, Parker replaced his feet on the table next to hers and started rubbing his feet against hers in a gentle but suggestive massage. No words or looks were exchanged for lingering minutes. Then he reached over and placed her hand into his and squeezed.

"Marilyn, this house needs to be home, not for a single man, but for a man and his wife, preferably, a newly-wed couple with a future in business as well as in life. Marilyn, I love you and I am asking you to consider making this a partnership for life. Will you marry me?"

More minutes passed with neither saying anything. Slowly, she turned toward him, wrapped his arms around her, and pressed their lips together for a long passionate kiss.

"Parker, I've read lots of romance novels in my day, but I have never heard nor read about a proposal like that. I do love you also, but you caught me a little . . . no, a lot off guard. Let me sleep on it and I will give you my answer tomorrow."

She encouraged another passionate kiss and then gently pushed him away.

"Take me home, Boss. This gal's got a lot of thinking to do; plus I got to report to work tomorrow."

CHAPTER SIXTEEN

Parker and Marilyn's Wedding

Early Friday morning, Parker arrived at his office as usual. However, his demeanor was not as usual. Having spent a restless night after proposing to Marilyn, he could hardly bring himself to face the fact that she did not seem overjoyed about the idea of a lifetime commitment.

What an ass I was, why didn't I wait for a more romantic setting? I should have picked a nice restaurant or a weekend trip to somewhere special. She surely is going to turn me down; and how do I handle that?

Eight o'clock, Eight-fifteen, Eight-thirty, and still no sign of Marilyn. And just as he decided he should call to check on her, Parker heard the back door open and the familiar click of the heels of her shoes on the hardwood hallway floor. Without pausing at her own desk, just outside of his office, she briskly strode into his office with her oversized purse and coat dangling over her arm.

"Morning Boss, sorry to be so late, but it took me quite a bit longer to get my act together this morning."

Parker could only sit there spellbound, just thinking how beautiful she looked standing there with the early sun shining through his window, as if she were a model in the spotlights of a runway. She was wearing an unusually tight-fitting skirt, part of a tasteful, beautiful, dark blue suit. Matching costume jewelry made the complete package.

Unable to speak coherently, he just half blurted out the words; "You look absolutely stunning, just absolutely stunning."

Smiling while listening, she replied: "Since I have not had a proposal before, well at least not a marriage proposal, I thought I had better shine up a bit for my acceptance speech. So, if I did not blow it with my hasty retreat last night, I would be most happy to accept your offer of teaming up as a business team as well as being the team of Mr. and Mrs. Parker Coburn."

Parker literally jumped from his chair and surrounded her with his arms, alternately kissing and hugging so violently that they both lost their balance and nearly fell to the floor. Stepping away from her for a minute, he raised his fist in a pumping fashion and loudly yelled: "Go Team."

Hearing the loud cry, Paul Hicks had rushed into Parker's office, fearful that something drastic had happened, and became the first to hear the news of their engagement and the first to extend congratulations.

The following three weeks was somewhere between total joy and total frustration for both Parker and Marilyn as they tried to deal with an unusual rush of company business and trying to find time to plan a wedding. In the relative short period of time, they had lived in Burson. The majority of the time had been involved with Parker's expanding business and little time for social activities in the community; hence, close friends outside of business customers and associates were few and far between. Neither of the two were enthusiastic about a large pretentious wedding, so, after a short discussion over dinner one evening at Palo's restaurant, a compromise was reached. They both wanted a church wedding, but with few guests and a small reception immediately following the ceremony. Parker was not a member of any church but had visited different local ones with the idea of joining the one he preferred, but just lacked the incentive to choose one over the other. Likewise, Marilyn also did not have membership in the church, but did frequently attend the First Baptist Church, with the largest congregation in this small West Texas town. Parker had no problem deferring to her choice of religion and suggested she make the necessary arrangements.

The following Sunday after the church service, Marilyn stayed a while after the minister had completely said his goodbyes and kind words to the many close brothers and sisters of his flock, and then asked for a private moment alone. The Reverend Tracy Sutton, a longtime icon of this church, was most accommodating. Motioning to a couple of plush but aging chairs in the now vacant hallway, he invited Marilyn to sit. Marilyn confided to Reverend Sutton their impending plans, and in spite that neither she nor Parker were members of any church, they both recognized the importance of their commitment to each other be with God's blessing.

Reverend Sutton listened intently and was most gracious and informative in his positive response. He not only agreed to conduct the ceremony, but also would arrange for the senior Bible class ladies to prepare and serve the refreshments in the fellowship hall following the ceremony.

The third Friday of this current month was agreed to as a date both the church and the minister would be available. The minister explained, when asked, no charges were expected for neither his service nor none would be expected for the refreshments donated by the Sunday school class.

Marilyn, near overcome by emotion with the kindness of Reverend Sutton, regained her composure and gathered her thoughts. Both she and Parker were doing well financially, she politely told the minister, and that a substantial donation would be forthcoming to the church and to the minister with their sincere appreciation for agreeing to oversee this milestone in their lives.

At 7:00 p.m. on Friday, September 19, 1969, with the small group of their company employees and spouses, a few business associates, and a few members of the Sunday school class that Marilyn attended, the vows were repeated, and the Reverend Tracy Sutton pronounced them husband and wife. After the groom had kissed the bride, the minister introduced the newlywed couple, Mr. and Mrs. Parker Coburn. Guests at the wedding were then invited to the reception in the adjoining fellowship hall.

The honeymoon began that same evening with a three hour drive to Dallas and a nice suite in a prominent downtown hotel. On Saturday, knowing Marilyn's taste for fine clothing, her wedding present was a no-limit shopping spree at Niemen Marcus, the most prestigious clothing store in Texas. However, also knowing Marilyn's passion for NFL football, a bonus wedding gift was two forty-yard-line tickets to her beloved Dallas Cowboys at Cowboy Stadium in Irving, Texas.

The honeymoon concluded with a late evening drive returning to Burson, where Mr. and Mrs. Parker Coburn spent their first night together in their new home at 213

East Sadosa Street. Monday morning would come much too soon, but work goes on, and on, and on.

CHAPTER SEVENTEEN

Parker and Marilyn's Surprising Decision

Parker and Marilyn Coburn, suddenly, only a little over two years after first opening the doors for business, the unthinkable happened. Without rumors or even signs of discontent, Parker called the office staff together and made a startling announcement. Marilyn would be leaving the company effective immediately. Their first and only marriage for both would be ending in a mutually agreed on divorce. Their marriage had been childless and that no infidelity problems, etc., was an issue or cause. He further stated that Marilyn had asked him to convey her gratitude to all on the staff, whom she considered to be good friends, and would be down in a couple of days to thank them personally. He extended his personal thanks and asked for their understanding of the delicate subject. Parker then dismissed the assembled group without additional explanation or dialogue.

The cause of the divorce, although no close friends or fellow employees ever knew for sure, was thought to be just the result of a ho-hum marriage; no real problems, just a divorce that the involved parties had agreed would most likely improve both of their lives. Marilyn, who had grown up in a metropolitan area with many upscale shops and restaurants and was seeking her future somewhere other than Burson, had requested the divorce.

Marilyn visited the office before leaving Burson with lots of hugs and handshakes and good-byes.

With an adequate financial settlement and having acquired a promising new job as well as a spacious comfortable apartment in Dallas, she optimistically began her adventure into a new way of life.

Parker and Marilyn each agreed to "stay in touch."

Chapter Eighteen

The Police Investigation, Second Meeting

Police Chief Ward Thompson had not even had time to place his hat on the hat rack before his private line was ringing aggressively, or so it seemed to be, on this Tuesday morning only a bit over a week since the murder of Bob Herring Jr.

"Chief Ward Thompson here," was his straight-forward introduction to the phone call.

"Ward, this is Buck. Not too sure how much work your boys have got done on the Herring case, but my guys have come up with a couple of things. Thought maybe it's time we sat and reviewed what we each got to date. You got any time today?"

"Sure Buck, I'll pretty well work it in anytime you say. We just got some information back from the Lab in Austin yesterday, but I'm not sure where it will lead us, if anywhere. We haven't been able to come up with much yet to get us going in any particular direction, but I will bring you up to date on our part, and I will be glad to hear what you came up with."

"Good . . . how 'bout one o'clock, my place?" Buck asked. "Fits my schedule, and I'll bring Phil along with me. He's the one that is sort of taking the lead on this case."

"Good, Ward, and I'll make sure Randy is also here. That boy's got a good nose for this sort of thing. See you after lunch."

Chief Thompson cradled the phone receiver and walked to the outer office to notify Randy of the appointment.

The black-and-white Dodge police car, driven by office Phil Hawkins and accompanied by Chief Ward Thompson, wheeled into one of the reserved parking spaces in front of Sheriff Buck Jones' office, just one block west of the County Court House, that was located on the square in downtown Burson. A large clock on the wall inside the receptionist's office indicated exactly 1 p.m. when Chief Ward and Phil entered.

"Good afternoon, Chief Thompson, Phil; Sheriff Jones is expecting you. Please go on in." The greeting was from Shirley Johnson, the pleasingly plump, salt and pepper graying haired receptionist that had been in her position for the four elected terms of Sheriff Jones and two previous terms of the former Sheriff.

"Thanks Shirley, I'll visit with you a little bit later. Buck and I got a little business to discuss."

Buck rose from his chair, and after a brief handshake and greeting with Ward and Phil, ushered them into the hallway toward the investigation room where Randy Spears was waiting. Buck had keys in hand as they approached the door, inserted the key, unlocked the door, and motioned for Ward and Phil to enter. As Randy rose to greet the two policemen, Buck spoke: "Probably a waste of my time to tell you both, as I'm sure that you both know it already, but just to keep it all in legal perspective, what you see and what we discuss stays in this room. OK?"

"Affirmative," replied Ward.

Randy and Phil both answered in agreement.

Randy had outlined the case on a large chalkboard. Dates, times, weather conditions, diagrams of the area of the murder scene, location of the body, trajectory of the bullet, and possible locations of the firing position of the murder suspect. Listed in the upper right-hand corner was a bullet report of possible motives. A separate but adjacent bulletin board was filled with several sheets of paper describing the biography of the victim, the family members, and other short bios of people of interest, all possible suspects. A nearby eight-foot table provided the space for various pieces of evidence, each clearly marked with a piece of white poster board placed underneath, with hand-written notes regarding how the evidence was gathered, etc.

The Police Chief and Officer Phil studied every item of evidence and info concerning the case that Deputy Randy Spears had accumulated and painstakingly outlined.

While examining a plaster cast of tire prints, Chief Thompson questioned: "You told me about these, Buck. Did you come up with anything on these tires?"

"Well, you know, it was raining a light drizzle that morning, so that pretty much wiped out anything real good that we had to look at. Randy found this one print, underneath a tree, that was pretty much protected from the moisture, but we did have enough for an ID. They turned out to be Firestone 310-225's, rain-thread. Trouble with that is, about every pickup in town has that same tire, seeing as how the Firestone store is the biggest tire store in town, and besides that, it probably wasn't even bought in this town."

Buck moved to another part of the evidence table and picked up another plaster cast; this one of a shoeprint. Handing the cast to Ward, he offered his opinion: "Randy's got several good prints like this in the area where we believe the suspect's vehicle was parked. However, this guy must have well thought this out, cause this ain't no normal shoe print."

"How, what do you mean, not normal?"

"Well, as near as we can figure out, this is a flat sole, no heel sandal or something like that. Also, from the indentations of cross weave, it looks as if the suspect wore heavy work-socks over the footwear to prevent the identification. And to add more to the confusion of the whole mess, Randy did a little testing of his own trying to ascertain the weight of the suspect. He went back the next day, while the weather conditions were about the same, and took a cast of his own footprint to determine if the depth of the imprint were deeper or shallower than his own; figured he could tell if the suspect was lighter or heavier than himself."

"And?" questioned Ward.

"Still gets more puzzling. Randy calculates the dude is a light weight, less than one hundred fifty pounds, but wears about a size thirteen shoe. Or in other words, a little person with extra big feet."

"Interesting," mused Chief Thompson, "from this persons of interest group, you got a lot of people I know, but I'm having trouble thinking anyone of those could do this. Heaven knows a lot of folks have been hurt enough to want to waste this guy, but to actually pull the trigger . . . that's a whole new ball game."

Deputy Randy Spears, who for the most part had been silent but had paid close attention to the conversation, decided to join in. "The list is mostly my doing, Chief. I put the names on the list simply because each one has been hurt by Herring's actions. In fact, both emotionally and financially. Besides that, a contract to get the job done is not out of the realm of possibility. A lot of murders are underwritten by someone who doesn't have the stomach to do the job themselves."

"Can't argue with your reasoning, Randy . . . Still, it's hard for me to conceive that anyone you have on that list, to date, could possibly be that angry at Herring, despite how much money they have been bilked out of."

Officer Phil Hawkins was meticulously pouring over the time and place details on the chalk board when Sheriff Buck Jones motioned for Ward Thompson to follow him into an adjacent room.

"Let Sherlock and Dr. Watson compare notes and bring each other up to date, Ward. I got something I want to discuss with you."

Once inside, he closed the door behind them and looked about to be assured of their privacy.

"Ward," he began, "Got something to share with you that I just found out. I know Randy like a son and trust him implicitly, but I don't know Phil that well. That's why I have something to tell you, strictly confidential, that only Randy and I and a couple of other folks know. After I tell you, then you can decide if you trust Phil enough to let him in on it."

"Phil has been with me about seven years now and, like your relationship with Randy, I'm sure he knows how to keep his mouth shut. However, let's hear what you got to say and then I'll decide if Phil should know or not."

Buck motioned toward a small interrogation desk with two wooden, unpadded chairs and the two law officers sat down, facing each other across the table. Buck began, but still wanting the assurance of not being overheard, leaned toward Ward and lowered his voice: "Randy visited Chat Cason yesterday morning down at the hospital. You surely have heard that Chat has been sort of in and out of it all week; it's been touch and go with him from the time of the accident. The doctor told me last week that these first few days are critical to his recovery. And even if he makes it, no one outside of God knows what his mental status will be."

"Yeah, I've heard much the same. Poor guy . . . and Joanie and those two little tykes, three or four or somewhere close to that. Just doesn't seem right for such a nice family."

Sheriff Buck said, still speaking in a low voice, "I agree wholeheartedly, just gotta pray for all of them." He paused before continuing, "Here's the kicker, though . . . Chat actually spoke to Randy for a few minutes before he went back into that sleep mode that he has been drifting in and out of. You know that Randy and Chat were surprisingly good buddies?"

"Yeah, I'd seen them hang out a bit together. Families were friends also, right?"

"Yes, at least, that's my understanding. Chat told Randy that Joanie had told him about what happened to Bob Herring on the same morning of his accident and that an investigation to find the assailant was underway. Said that he'd been thinking about that and he thought he might know something about a possible suspect. Randy said he began to get very emotional just thinking about it, and had a real hard time talking about it. Apparently, he was looking back toward the old Herring Ranch road and what we think was the suspect's car and that was what caused his accident. Said the last thing he remembered was someone obviously trying to get out of sight behind their truck. The whole thing looked really suspicious to him and diverted attention away from his driving."

Police Chief Thompson could no longer stand the wait and interrupted Buck's slow dissertation, "Did he know who it was? Was he able to give Randy a name?"

"No, no way we could be that lucky, but he did say there was no way he could be positive about the identity of the person attempting to hide; but was pretty dang sure he recognized the pickup."

Ward, again, could not contain his enthusiasm, "Great, have you checked it out?"

"Hold your horses, Ward. You should know by now no murder is that easily solved. The sad truth is . . . that's the last words Chat spoke. He slipped back into a deep sleep, and this time the doc is not too optimistic about whether this might be just another short one or is the big sleep. Doc said we'll just have to pray and wait it out."

"So, Buck, to sum it up, Chat may the key to identifying the killer, but may never recover enough to tell us who he is."

"That's the way I see it; and that's why I think we need to keep this on the QT. I can think of a lot of folks that's got motives and probably are not unhappy about his untimely passing, but most of them are just not capable of going through with anything that drastic. If someone really hated Herring enough to do him in, they may just want to cover their tracks by making sure that Chat never wakes up. You know, if it were a professional hit, bought and paid for, then it's not logical that Chat would have recognized the pickup. But on the other hand, whether it is or not someone local that put in that much planning and work to do the job and not reveal any clues to their identity, they might not hesitate to do one more to protect their secret. That's my main reason for as few as possible knowing what I told you. I just don't think we can take the chance with Chat's life."

Police Chief Ward was deep in thought and took several moments to frame his response before speaking: "Point taken. I'm going to think this over before saying anything to Phil. In fact, I probably won't say anything to anyone just now; let it simmer for a bit and see what happens. I do think I'm going to do a little research on this "who's got a motive" angle and see what I can come up with. I'll get back to you on that and maybe compare notes in about a week. Got anything else? If not, I better get back to the office."

Sheriff Jones, pushing his chair back from the desk: "Nope, that's it for me. I wanted you to see what little evidence the boys had put together, but this little conversation was the main reason I wanted you here in person. Have yourself a good day, Ward . . . and thank you for the cooperation."

"If any thanks are in order, it's from me to you. See you around!"

CHAPTER NINETEEN

Parker Interviews Betty Jean Morrison

Betty Jean Morrison, a young, vibrant, recent college graduate of Hardin Simmons University in nearby Abilene, entered the small parking lot adjacent to the Coburn Oil & Gas Company at 8:30 in the morning on June 12th, 1972. The only child of Barton and Nancy Morrison had spent her entire life growing up in the small historic town of Eastland, only a few miles from where she graduated from college. Her loving parents still owned and operated a small mom-and-pop business that had supported the small family, not pretentiously, but adequately, throughout her childhood. Neither her Mother nor Father, both reared from low income but hard-working families, had attended college. Therefore, they were especially proud, as are all parents, of their daughter's graduation in the top ten percent of her class, but even more proud of the clean wholesome young Christian lady they had successful reared.

The classified ad from the Abilene Sentinel, neatly clipped, in a small white envelope without a return address, had arrived the past Monday. The stick-on return address

had apparently inadvertently peeled off as the adhesive blur was still evident. The ad for a personal secretary had stated oil and gas industry experience was preferred but would not rule out recent college or business school graduates. Always the eternal optimist, she had taken the initiative and called, requesting a personal interview instead of mailing in her resume. Being thirty minutes early and assured of being punctual for her scheduled 9:00 a.m. appointment, she spent fifteen minutes checking makeup, touching up her hair, and gathering her thoughts.

This is it, time to go girl . . . and . . . think positively.

Mrs. Patton, an employee of Temporary Help, Inc., notified Parker of the job applicant's arrival.

"Mr. Coburn will see you shortly." Motioning to a guest chair, she asked: "Could I get you a cup of coffee while you wait?"

"No, I'm fine, but thank you very much."

She was barely seated before Parker Coburn, president and sole owner of the company, strode briskly into the reception area.

"Parker Coburn, Miss Morrison. May I call you Betty? Or is it Betty Jean?"

"Either one is fine, but if I get a vote, I prefer Betty Jean; or if you prefer, simply Betty. I answer to both."

"Great," he replied, pausing while extending his hand toward his office. "Please come in."

After a few minutes scanning Betty Jean's résumé, Parker launched into an in-depth explanation of the company history. Day by day operations, expected growth, pay, and benefits etc., were all topics covered in the discussion. Betty Jean listened attentively and only interrupted a couple of times, asking pertinent questions.

The staff of the small independent company consisted of only five full-time office personnel, not counting Parker himself, who not only served as president, but "jack of all trades." There was a full time geologist with his assistant, a lease administrator, with his combination assistant–secretary, and the now vacant position as Parker's personal secretary. Other than the full-time office staff, there were contract employees manning positions of pumpers, truck drivers, mechanics, and lease salesmen.

During this initial interview, Parker promised the applicant, that if offered the secretarial position and she accepted, she could also begin training in lease management, making use of her newly earned business degree.

Another twenty-five minutes of question-and-answer dialogue was abruptly ended as Parker Coburn arose from his chair, turned to gaze out of his office window for a moment, and then returned his attention to the beautiful young lady seated directly in front of his desk.

"Speaking generally, I don't make hasty decisions on something that is this important to me. But, Miss Morrison, you are a very impressive young lady! I would love to have you come to work for my company. In fact, so much so, I'll up the starting salary I discussed with you a few minutes ago by a hundred dollars a month. What do you say?"

She was attempting to curb her enthusiasm and remain somewhat calm, but the pure excitement of being offered such a potentially great job on her first interview was too much to conceal. No longer able to hold back the streaming tears of joy, she leaped to her feet and extended her hand for the acceptance handshake. "Yes . . . and thank you so very much. I won't let you down. When do I start?"

"That's up to you Betty Jean, but for my part, yesterday was too late." He laughed slightly and added, "More seriously, take what time you need to get it done. I'm sure you'll need to find an apartment or something. I'll introduce you to the other office folks and I'm sure that they can help with that. Shall we set next Monday as a target date? My temporary help is good through this week."

"Monday is great. I'll make sure of that," Betty Jean confirmed. "Follow me, let's go meet the gang."

Chapter Twenty

Betty Jean's First Six Months on the Job

The first six months in the office of Parker Coburn's oil and gas company was a mixture of bliss and frustration for the newest employee, Betty Jean Morrison. She loved her job and the part of her duties that were primarily being Parker's personal secretary was snap for the young, intellectual, recent ACC graduate. The frustrating part of her new career mostly occurred while training to handle the rather complicated legal end of the leasing business, the training that Parker had promised when he had employed her. The task had become almost mind numbing with the many forms required to be filled out weekly, and recorded along with endless copies and royalty checks to be mailed to investors, as well as seemingly hundreds of reports to the oil and gas commission.

Most companies, large and small, utilize the standard forty-hour work week as a normal practice for their employees. Sometimes though, smaller companies are often staffed by ones who become more friends than fellow workers, and usually are fiercely loyal to each other as well as to the owner, who often doubles as the manager. That loyalty leads to more dedication to getting the job done, and that in turn often leads to a disregard for standard work hours. That dedication led to a late-night working session of two of the Coburn Oil & Gas Company's office staff, Parker and Betty Jean.

It was a 5:15 one Friday afternoon in March as Parker exited his office and stopped at Betty Jean's desk. Her office, not really an office in the general sense, consisted of a nice walnut desk, a row of file cabinets, and a separate small desk housing a printer as well as other business machines. A still smaller table was in the corner that was home for the always present coffee maker and condiments. This reality, the small group of office furniture arranged as in a cubicle, was all part of a larger lobby and entrance to the office building.

Parker spoke, "Hey Bet," the new nickname that she had been pinned by a fellow worker and had stuck. "You got anything going tonight so important that you can't get out of? You know, like a hot date that won't wait?"

"Oh, absolutely, with all these dozens of eligible handsome bachelors in Burson pursuing me, I can scarcely find an empty space in my calendar." The mischievous smile gave into a more serious expression: "Of course, nothing is more important than my boss's needs. What do you need me to do?"

"Matter of fact is, I got one hell of a lot of contracts that have to be in the mail Monday morning. I was sort of hoping that you might work over and help me finish." Anticipating a positive answer, he quickly added, "We can pick up some burgers and shakes from the Dairy Queen, or order in a pizza if you like!"

It had been a long day, a long work week, and she had really been looking forward to a hot shower, a frozen dinner, and good book to read. But unhesitatingly, and in an almost musical voice declared, "You know," he said and then paused, "it's sort of like taking one for the team. Count me in, captain, and I like everything on my burger. Lots of fries, lots of ketchup, and make the milkshake chocolate and extra thick."

Parker had come to appreciate Bet's quick wit and always present smile. He was silently patting himself on the back for his good judgment in hiring this young vivacious ACC graduate. "What a find," he mumbled to himself, and then in a louder tone: "Great, I'm off for the burgers. Do your own thing for the next fifteen or so; this burger man will be back like jack in a flash."

Less than thirty minutes later and carrying two large sacks, the newest Dairy Queen delivery boy entered through the front door, transferred both food sacks to one hand, and turned to snap the dead bolt in place. Bet had already cleared space on her desk for eating and had brought in a roll of paper towels from the nearby storage room. She was pushing one of the office guest-chairs toward her desk when Parker commanded: "No, no, my office! I've got the conference table that's much larger and the guest chairs in my office are more comfortable. Come on in and bring the paper towels. Good idea, 'cause these burgers are really juicy."

The next thirty minutes was the scene of a couple of hungry co-workers eating their fill, idle chit chat, and a genuine sense of appreciation; one for the other. And in that thirty-minute food break a new relationship, more than just that of a boss and his secretary, was formed, and all with burgers and fries.

Both Parker and Bet were feeling uneasy and somewhat embarrassed, the result of increasingly frequent eye contact. As a self-reprimand, Parker forced himself to shelve the unthinkable thoughts pouring into his mind. Picking up the trash from the table, he changed the tone of the conversation by stating: "Okay, dinner's over and hi ho, hi ho, it's off to work we go. Grab those Gallagher and Dempsey contracts, Bet, and your steno pad. Let's get after it. It's going to be a long night."

Shortly after midnight, two exhausted but dedicated workers laid down the completed contracts, gathered their personal belongings, and left the building. Parker escorted Betty Jean to her car and once she was safely inside, offered, "Good night, Betty Jean. You were sensational tonight, good work. Have a great weekend, get some rest. And I owe you one."

"You owe me nothing Parker, remember, it's all for the team." Laughingly she added, "seriously, just working for you is rewarding enough. I'm still in your debt for just hiring me. Good night to you also, and don't let the bed bug's bite. Ha, ha! Nighty-nite!" She backed out of her parking space and drove away into the darkness.

Parker paused for a moment of reflection while recalling the evening and the experience. He then entered his own car and began what was now a lonely journey home.

She's twenty-one or maybe twenty-two, and I'm thirty-two. Is that too much difference?

Chapter Twenty-One

Parker and Betty Jean's First Date

Almost exactly one year to date from Betty Jean's first day of employment, near the end of the normal day at work, Parker walked from his office to his secretary's desk, pulled up a chair and leaned back, almost reclining.

"You look as if you've been sent for and couldn't go," she said with obvious pleasure at her own analogy of his exhausted posture.

Not even bothering to lift his head he responded, "Tough day in the trenches; it's been one of those days, you know? At least, you ought to. I'm sure you heard enough of those telephone conversations, even though you could only hear my side, to figure out that this was one frustrating day."

Faking contempt with her facial expression, she curtly replied, "How dare you accuse me of eavesdropping. I would never stoop to such a level. However, since you spent half the day yelling at the top of your voice, I, as well as everyone walking down the street, could hear you quite clearly."

Raising his body to a sitting position, he acknowledged, "I suppose one might conclude, logically, that I was a bit agitated from time to time. Sometimes I wonder if some of

those idiots I work with are playing with a full deck? Oh, hell, it might just be me, who knows. Anyway, that's done for now, in the past, on to greener pastures."

"It feels good to let off the steam every now and then, doesn't it?" Betty Jean said.

"Yes, and speaking of that, I know just how to do it! Let off steam, that is. I got me a great idea. Interested?" Parker asked.

"Depends."

"On what?"

"On your definition of letting off steam, of course," she offered.

"You mean, after a whole year, you have finally figured out that I've been hitting on you?" he said.

Betty Jean then lowered her head, raised her eyebrows, and in her best imitation of a southern drawl, "Well, I do declare, Mr. Coburn, are you insinuating that you are not the total southern gentleman you've been portraying?"

He returned with his attempt at Clark Gable, "Frankly, Scarlett, I don't give a damn." Leaning forward in his chair, he continued in his normal voice, "Actually, I'm no Clark Gable, and probably not too much of a gentleman either. But I do have a plan, and if you would accompany me, I will promise to be on my best behavior."

Also returning to her normal voice, she flashed a quick smile and replied, "Parker, you surely know that exchange was all in good fun. You are truly a gentleman, and I respect you very much. And, if I don't seem too forward, I also like you very much."

"That goes double for me, Bet. Now am I to interpret that as an affirmative answer to my offer for the evening?" Parker asked.

"Still depends, but I'm more than willing to listen to the offer."

"Fair enough, you like football?"

"Do chickens lay eggs? Of course. Wasn't I born and bred in West Texas? Who doesn't like football?"

"Well, it is Friday, and Whistler's got his final spring scrimmage game tonight. I haven't missed one in several years and the whole town will be there. I'm sure that you've heard about it. Couldn't live in Burson and not know about it."

"Sounds exciting, count me in. Do I meet you there, or what?" Betty Jean asked.

Looking at his watch, he ran a quick mental calculation and offered, "Let's see, it's five-twenty now, and the game starts at seven-thirty. Can you be home and get yourself into some football fan gear by six-forty-five? If so, and if you're okay with it, I'll run home and shower, change, and swing by your place and pick you up about six forty-five. That will get us to the stadium about seven and we can grab some hot dogs and sodas at the concession stand to tide us over. And, still assuming you do not find me too offensive, we can eat properly after the game. Several of the restaurants always stay open late on game nights."

"Sounds like a man with a plan. I'll be ready at six forty-five, and I am looking forward to it," Betty Jean said.

Only a couple of minutes before seven o'clock, Parker paid for three hot dogs, two bags of potato chips, and two large size Dr. Pepper's at the Bobcat Stadium concession stand. He then left a generous tip in the tip bottle and escorted Betty Jean to the home side thirty-yard line seats. The stadium, seating capacity eight thousand, was already more than half-full for this annual Blue–White game. The Blue team first-string offense and second-string defense versus the White team first-string defense and second-string offense, was traditionally the game signifying the formal end of spring training. Generous donations from the Booster Club, contributed largely to Whistler Williams' coaching success in past years, had kept the old Bobcat Stadium in tip top shape, even providing seat backs in all but the end zone seating areas.

Parker had finished both of his hot dogs and more than half of his soda before Betty Jean had eaten half of hers.

"Boy, are you slow, or what?" Parker asked jokingly. "Unlike your mother, my mother did not let me eat with the pigs," she retorted in jest.

Both laughed heartily. The earlier awkward uneasiness between the two, present at the beginning of this first date, faded as the evening edged on toward game time.

The Offense and Defensive teams were in their final warm-up drills when Whistler Williams strolled over to the rail where Parker and Betty Jean were seated. Leaning on the rail, Coach Williams extended a warm handshake to Parker. "Good to see you Parker; missed seeing you at practice this year."

"Sorry, Coach. Had more irons in the fire than I could handle this past couple of months. Surely hated to miss the practices, but I've been hearing good things about the team. What do you think? Can we go all the way again this year?"

Pausing to look back at his team for a minute and after yelling at a young receiver for dropping a pass, he returned his attention to Parker, "You sure as hell know me better than that, Parker. We got to get the first one in the win column, and then the second etc. Like all the smart ones opine, one game at a time." He then turned his attention to Betty Jean but continued speaking to Parker, "I know the name of this pretty young lady, but we've not been formally introduced."

"Whistler, Betty Jean Morrison. Betty Jean, Coach Whistler Williams, the greatest high school coach in all of Texas. Betty Jean is my secretary, formally from Abilene, and tonight, I'm showing her what a real high school football team looks like."

Betty Jean initiated the greeting by quickly leaning over the rail and extended a firm handshake accompanied by a beautiful smile. "It's a pleasure to meet you, Coach Williams. I've heard nothing but good things about you. I'm looking forward to the game."

"Betty Jean, the pleasure belongs to me. You're even prettier up close and in person. I had previously only seen you from a distance." Turning to Parker, "Why don't you bring her over for dinner some evening soon? I would like for Betty Jo to meet her. I think they would hit it off good. She would enjoy Betty Jo's cooking, that's for sure. I'll have her call you soon and set up a date. No . . . is not an option."

One of the assistant coaches had whistled, signaling the end of the warm-up drills, and the teams hustled off the field to receive their final pep talk prior to the start of the game. The fans were alive with pre-game enthusiasm. Coach Whistler waved to Parker and Betty Jean as he trotted off the field behind his young warriors. The game was only minutes away.

The game proved to be as exciting as Parker had promised, with a last-minute winning score.

Trailing 20 to 14 and backed up to their own ten-yard line, the Blue team had fumbled on a handoff to their senior starting running-back and a defensive tackle for the White team recovered the ball on the three. There was only thirty-three seconds left on the field clock when the referee stopped the clock for the change of possession rule. Two running plays later, with a time out sandwiched in between, the White team scored the tying touchdown. The clock expired as the place kicker calmly kicked the extra point for the final score, 21 to 20, in favor of the White.

The crowd of fans roared their approval for both squads and surged onto the playing field to congratulate both teams. Neither team, Blue nor White, was a loser on this beautiful May evening.

It was shortly after 10:00 p.m., indicated by the illuminated dash clock in Parker's Chevrolet Suburban, when Parker and Betty Jean pulled into the slow-moving traffic exiting the Bobcat Stadium.

Patting her gently on the knee, Parker asked, "Okay, I promised a real dinner after the game. Where would you like to eat?"

"To be perfectly honest, that hot dog, chips, and huge soda just about done me in. And that does not even account for the popcorn we devoured later. Fact is, I'd settle for something light and call it a night."

The traffic backup began to open up a bit and Parker accelerated the Suburban toward Main Street.

"Sounds good to me, and I got myself a brilliant idea. Seeing as how neither you nor I have to watch our diet too closely, how's about a super thick milkshake from the Dairy Queen? I do believe I remember you like chocolate."

"That's perfect," she said, and with a personal pat on the back, "I even amaze myself sometimes when my cunning plans work to perfection."

"You mean you were working me, huh?" Parker asked. "Working you? You must be joking. I wouldn't dare work you, Parker Coburn. After all, you're my boss."

Both erupted in laughter as they headed for the Dairy Queen.

Deciding to skip the formalities of dining inside amid what seemed to be dozens of high school students in celebration following the game, Parker had chosen the drive-in window to purchase the milkshakes. Sipping slowly, and driving slowly as well, he made his way to Betty Jean's apartment. She had located this duplex, two apartments side by side, mirror images of each other, the same week that she had accepted the job with Parker. Luckily, it had only been recently vacated and she was able to secure a one-year lease with only one-month payment in advance. Two small bedrooms, a combination den and living area, kitchen, and bath more than met her needs as a single working girl. There was also a front porch with a porch swing, and a small front and back yard, maintained by the owners, who lived in the adjacent apartment. The owners, Dale and Mildred Atkins, were in their late seventies, extremely nice, and minded their own business. The leased apartment provided the additional income they needed to supplement the Social Security checks essential to their retirement.

Two huge hackberry trees, one in front of each apartment, provided cover and shade for the front yard. A small driveway with a carport attached to the building on either side provided parking. Betty Jean's Pontiac was under the carport as Parker wheeled into a parking spot under the hackberry in front of the apartment. Switching off the headlights, Parker was unsure of what his next move should be. Neither one had finished their dairy treats, and neither one had the inclination to end the evening. They sat in relative silence, each waiting for the other to speak for several moments, seemingly content to enjoy the cold milkshake and the exquisite beauty of the evening.

With a bright moon playing hide-and-seek with the branches of the old hackberry tree, now at night providing darkness instead of daylight shade, the evening seemed to be perfect for romance. Any thoughts of this night ending by fulfilling one of his fantasy dreams involving Betty Jean came to a sudden halt as she broke the extended silence.

"Parker," she began, "I truly do not want to burst your bubble, but I don't have to be psychic to know what you're thinking. Truthfully, I'm probably thinking the same thing you are thinking. I would love to invite you in, but although Mr. and Mrs. Atkins would never say anything to me about it, I know they would not approve. Furthermore, both my mom and my dad, from day one, have drilled into my head the danger of a young single girl becoming infatuated with their boss. I'm really hoping that you understand."

Parker squirmed uncomfortably before speaking, in a slow and thoughtful reply, "Bet, I could not deny that some crazy things have crossed my mind in the last few minutes. But surely you know me well enough by now, I would never—I mean never—do anything to purposefully upset you. I have way too much respect for you for that. I'm not at all sure what you expect me to say now, but I hope you're not telling me that this means never."

She started to interrupt when he continued, "Please let me finish my thought before you tell me more."

She nodded her approval.

"It's just been a year now, but I've observed you closely. I watch the way you interact with people, how nice and polite you are, how professional you are with your work, and your morals and habits are above reproach. Add all of that to your out of this world sexy looks, and your always upbeat personality, earns you a rating of a perfect ten."

She again started to reply when he again asked, "Please, just a bit more of my thinking. I fully realize that we have an age difference, roughly twelve years, and that has to be a bigger problem for you than for me. I also know that I carry some baggage, a previous marriage, but I think we, Marilyn and l, did the right thing about that. So, to sum it up in a nutshell, I'm trying, in my feeble ways with words, to say I care for you, much more than you could possibly know. Another way to put it, I am not just out looking for a one-night stand. I will be most pleased if you consider this expression of my feelings for you as seriously as I offered them."

Betty Jean was overcome with emotion. The sincerity in his voice and amplified by his demeanor caused a flow of tears from her beautiful blue eyes. She could barely resist the temptation created in that moment. Her inclination was to wrap her arms around him and kiss him passionately, but more rational thoughts fought their way into her head.

Steady girl, steady. Keep your head on straight. Sounds wonderful, but think this out. Don't just sit here like an awestruck teenager, say something.

Parker had offered her his handkerchief, which she accepted. "Thank you," she said.

After dabbing her eyes dry, she returned the handkerchief, "Thank you again." She paused again before continuing: "Parker, that has to be one of the most beautiful expressions of someone's feelings that I have ever heard. I appreciate everything you have said, and I totally believe you meant it, every word of it. You've put a lot on my plate to think about, but I promise that I will consider what you said. And as you requested, I will absolutely do it seriously."

She then leaned closer, took both of his hands in hers, clasped them tightly, pulled him toward her, and kissed him affectionately on the cheek. She purposefully held the kiss for several seconds. Pushing back away from him, she paused, then pulled him close to her body again and placed a second kiss on the cheek, briefly this time, and whispered, "I do care for you too, very much. Thanks for a wonderful evening. The milkshake was fabulous. Good night!!"

She twisted in her seat to open the door, and before Parker could possibly exit his door to open it for her, had exited the car, closed the door, and walked rapidly to her apartment. She paused only long enough to turn and wave good night. After feeling assured that she was safely inside her apartment, Parker started the engine, switched on the headlights, and started the ten-minute drive to his home.

He could not help but be pleased with the outcome of the evening.

CHAPTER TWENTY-TWO

Betty Jean Meets Bob Herring Jr. for the First Time

"Good morning, pretty lady, you must be the new kid on the block I heard about." Bob Herring Jr. spoke as he visually sized up the attractive young blonde behind her desk in the outer office, just outside of Parker Coburn's private office. And without waiting for the reply, "Come to think of it, I suppose you're not all that new. Been about a year, right?" And without waiting for the answer, he proceeded, "Damn, that Parker sure got an eye for good lookers, girl, you've got it in spades. What are you doing tonight?"

And good looking she was! Because she had been pretty, in fact beautiful would be the more accurate way to describe her, she had long since learned to fend off the male Romeo types without losing her cool. Ignoring his flirtatious remarks and sticking strictly to business, she politely replied, "And how may I help you, sir?"

Slightly stunned by the obvious put-down, he paused for a moment before answering, "Sorry, I didn't mean to offend you. I was just kidding, you know. Is Parker in?"

"Yes, may I take your name, please? I will ask if he'll see you."

"Bob Herring. Most folks call me 'Little Bob.' I'm a Junior, you know."

"Thank you, Mr. Herring." She picked up the phone and announced, "Mr. Coburn, a Mr. Bob Herring Jr. would like to speak with you." After a short pause, she said, "Mr. Coburn told me to have you just come on in."

She smiled faintly as he tipped his hat and briskly strode into the adjoining office. Betty Jean's first meeting with one of the town's most eligible bachelors wasn't as unpleasant or unemotional as she had portrayed. Privately, there was a rather warm feeling of attraction, that of a physical nature, to the quite handsome and somewhat flirty man she had just met. Although she was keenly aware of whom he was and the hundreds of rumors about his shady dealings, he was also known for his outgoing personality. And many of the single ladies around town, and some married ones as well, were attracted to this young rich playboy with the boyish grin, irresistible charm, and bad boy image.

Am I really thinking what I'm thinking? I know he is not married. I wonder if he has a steady girlfriend. Gosh, he was pretty danged cute. Wonder if he comes in here much. Oh well, get over it, girl, back to work.

Forty minutes later Bob Jr. emerged from Parker's office, stopped, turned around and with a wave of his hat, "Get back to you in a few days on that, Park. I'll check it out with my guy when I see him later this week." Turning around to direct his attention to Betty Jean, he added a postscript to his farewell, "If this secretary works as good as she looks, Park, you got a keeper. Is she available or do you have her social calendar all booked up?"

Smiling that well discussed boyish grin at the secretary that was the center of his attention. "No disrespect, Miss Morrison, just joshing you and Park. It was real nice to meet you and hope to see you soon. Parker and I may have a couple of more business deals in the cooker, so I will probably be around quite frequently. I wish you a very pleasant day."

"Nice to meet you, too, Mr. Herring. You enjoy your day also." That was the words from her mouth but in her inner thoughts: *Gosh, I think I understand the bad rich playboy attraction the gal's gossip about. There is, for sure, sort of an animal attraction about him, one sexy dude.*

Tuesday morning of the following week, Betty Jean was digging through file cabinets in the storeroom adjoining her office. The all too familiar ring of the telephone, as it always does when you are out of reach, continued the monotonous monotone. It had rung numerous times before she was able to return to her desk, lift the receiver, and answer. "Mr. Coburn's office, may I help you?"

"Bob Herring Jr., Miss Morrison. How are you today?" "Very well, thank you. Sorry to keep you waiting. I was searching for some contracts in the file room. I assumed one of the others would pick up."

"No problem," Bob said. "Is Parker in?"

"No, I'm sorry. He and the geologist went to the county courthouse to look up something or the other. He said they would have lunch before they returned. Can I be of any help?"

"Of course, I would love to say yes, but in this case, I suppose this has to do with me and Parker. But you know what, how about me treating you to lunch? Like, you know, the mouse can play, while the cat's away."

Her emotions were a mixture of partially being pleased and flattered, but a bit indignant of his painfully obvious attempt to hit on her. What did he think she was, some cheap pick-up?

Regaining her composure, she politely replied, "That's nice of you, but I have my tuna sandwich and a small salad in our fridge. I seldom eat lunch out, but again, thank you. Shall I tell Mr. Coburn you called, or would you like to leave a message?"

"Just tell him I called and get back to me when he can. He knows how to reach me." And then in an apologetic tone, "Sorry if I came on a little too much about the lunch. I sometimes tend to get a bit too cute, a bad habit of mine. I'll do better in the future. Take care now!"

"Everything is fine, Mr. Herring. I'll tell him you called, and good-bye."

Two, with quite different personalities, were contemplating the circumstances of past few minutes of discussion. Completely opposite opinions were working through the minds of Bob Jr. and Betty Jean as he left the office. Bob Jr. was convinced he had made inroads toward winning the affection of the gorgeous young secretary and was looking forward to a more productive relationship. On the other hand, Betty Jean was thinking she had handled the situation well, professionally, and personally. She was not buying this line he was attempting to sell.

Chapter Twenty-Three

Who is Little Bob Herring?

The Herring Ranch, listed as a bit over eleven thousand acres on the tax rolls spread across two counties, approximately two-thirds in one and one-third in the other. Herring Cattle Ranch was the official listing in the court records, but oil production, exploration, and sales were the primary source of income to the Herring enterprise. Bob Sr. had initiated the oil exploration end of the business after first purchasing a used clean-out rig and contracting cleaning and re-drilling operations to the local oil producing companies. As the old producing wells begin to fade away, primarily because of old age and excessive pumping, business for the Herring services became more demanding, resulting in the purchase of more machinery, trucks, and dozens of employees. The financial success of the company was swiftly becoming a reality.

To his credit, Bob Sr. was determined to groom his only child, a son, from an early age to become a responsible heir to the family business by requiring him to work each summer along with regular company laborers. He was adamant in his

belief that no special treatment was to be given just because he was a Herring. He would not become just another spoiled, rich brat raised with a silver spoon in his mouth. Along with the hard manual work, there was a constant positive influence from both of his parents teaching politeness and respect.

Bob and Lillian Herring had to be proud of their young teenager as he breezed through his three years of high school. Although he was undersized for football, and not a stand-out athlete, he worked hard and earned the respect of coaches and team members alike for his contributions and dedication to team play. He excelled in the classroom, a constant member of the honor roll, and was elected student president in his senior year.

Other than excelling in curricular activities, he was also king of the hill with the young ladies. His better than average looks and overpowering personality easily made him the most wanted date in school by the young girls in Burson High. His good looks and charm were also aided significantly by the fact that he drove the hottest car in town, a new Red Chevrolet convertible. The car had been a gift from his mom and dad during his senior year, a reward for his scholastic achievements.

But the same outstanding traits that created many memorable high points in his romantic interludes with numerous pretty, perky young classmates also brought him to the lowest point in his young life. Rosa Marie Rodriguez, at sixteen, almost seventeen, a Hispanic beauty, was a relatively new student in the junior class. Her family had only moved into the area within the past few months, and she, along with two younger brothers, had enrolled into the local school system. As with so many young Hispanic ladies, her beauty was undeniable. Her long flowing black locks and beautiful, black haunting eyes, coupled with a perfect ten figure, brought longing stares from all the young bucks on campus. But it was young, personable Bob Herring Jr. that was the first to succeed in securing an affirmative answer for a date. And that date was only after a required personal visit with her parents, Palo and Rita Rodriquez, to secure their permission.

Bob Jr. and Rosa Marie soon became the hottest couple in school. The two never seemed to be far apart. Shared lunch breaks along with in-between class hallway meetings were common daily. He was always there to drive her home from school, and although she was not permitted to date on school nights, every weekend was a special evening in their lives. Young love was in full bloom.

CHAPTER TWENTY-FOUR

The Long Drive to Lubbock

Only three weeks into the summer session, Rosa Marie convinced her mother and father to let her accompany Bob Jr. on an outing to Lubbock, Texas. The announced reason for the all-day venture was Bob Jr.'s interest in attending Texas Tech University, and he simply wanted to visit the campus and check out potential dorm or apartment locations. Mom Rita was comfortable in the decision to let her now seventeen-year-old make the trip, but Papa Pablo took a lot more convincing.

Rosa Marie's big hug and kiss finally won him over and he reluctantly gave his approval, but only after assurances that she would be home before midnight.

The wind-up alarm clock on the small nightstand next to Pablo's bed increasingly became louder with each second that passed twelve o'clock midnight. The slight ticking was beginning to sound like a hammer beating on an anvil as an uncertain fear crowded his thoughts. He had complete trust in his only daughter's word, but this was not like her at all. Something had to be wrong, and he could only lay there and

anxiously wait for the sound of an approaching car, and the anticipated relief that only a teenager's parent can feel with their son or daughter's safe arrival home.

The sharp ring of the telephone drowned out the ticking sound of the clock and Pablo quickly rose to a sitting position and jerked the telephone receiver to his ear. A moment later, his worst fears were confirmed by a doctor calling from a small clinic in Lubbock. The father's heart and spirits sank as the doctor outlined the details of the day's events. An abortion procedure on Rosa Marie had turned bad, and due to excessive bleeding that he was unable to control, she was now in near critical condition. He was urging the parents to come as quickly as possible as he was transferring her to the Lubbock Memorial Hospital. Further explanation included the reason for the late hour notification. The patient and her boyfriend had both discouraged his calling her parents, hoping that she would get better soon and not be forced to reveal her pregnancy. He offered directions to the hospital and his sincere regrets of the outcome of the abortion surgery. Both he and Bob Jr. would be staying with her at the hospital until they arrived.

Pablo and Rita Rodriguez pulled into the emergency room parking lot of Lubbock Memorial Hospital after a less than three-hour drive from their home in Burson. After checking with the receptionist, they were quickly escorted to a surgical waiting room where they were greeted by a distraught Bob Herring Jr. Before he could offer much of an explanation to the worried parents, a hospital volunteer approached and asked: "Are you Miss Rodriguez's parents?" After the affirmative answer, she notified them that Dr. Bryan Wilkerson would like to meet with them in his office.

Fifteen minutes later, the same hospital volunteer answered the phone at her desk. After listening intently for a few moments in which she only responded with: "Yes, I understand" several times, she hung up the receiver and signaled to Bob Herring Jr. to come to her desk. The message was short and to the point. Sadly, Rose Marie had not survived the surgery, despite a gallant effort by two surgeons. Dr. Wilkerson was with the parents, who were emotionally broken, and he thought it best if they were left alone. He had asked to speak with Bob Jr. alone, not in the presence of her parents, because of their personal request. The volunteer was to escort him to an alternate office, where he could rest until the Doctor was comfortable that Palo and Rita had regained their composure.

After meeting with Dr. Wilkerson, filled with guilt and remorse, Bob Jr. had no one to turn to and nowhere to go. Despite his urgent request to meet with Pablo and Rita, the Doctor had assured him that the meeting would be more harmful than good. The parents' feeling toward Bob Jr. at this time was of total hostility, and it was the Doctor's recommendation that he should give them time to stem their anger before offering explanations or apologies. After grudgingly acceding to the Doctor's advice, he departed the small office and slowly made his way to his car, now early in the morning, in a near empty parking lot.

The speedometer of the Chevrolet convertible was registering only about forty miles-per-hour as Bob Jr. made his way back to his home in Burson. The wind in his face, with the top of the convertible being retracted, was calming some of his uneasiness as he approached Burson just at sunrise. After three plus hours of soul searching, along with fifty different scenarios in which he tried to absolve his own blame for what had happened, he still could not come up with a plausible storyline. Truth be known, it was he, and he alone, that pushed for the abortion. Primarily because of her religious upbringing and her strong right-to-life belief, Rose Marie had objected from the beginning. But, due to his insistence, having the baby and raising the boy or girl as a single parent would be more difficult than what he conceived to be the easy way out for both. "Marriage was out of the question," he had stated to her emphatically.

Still undecided as to what explanation to offer his parents, he parked his car in the driveway of the Herring Ranch home and slowly walked to the front door.

What the hell, why not just tell the truth? It will come out eventually. Maybe Mom and Dad will understand.

Chapter Twenty-Five

Pablo Rodriguez's Journey to the United States

Raul Rodriguez, a Minister of an Episcopal Church in Mexico for several years, was offered and accepted a similar position, but for a much larger Methodist Church in the border town of Brownsville, Texas. After several weeks of paperwork required to get a work permit and legally enter the United States, Raul and his family, wife Bianca and three young children, were finally settled in their new Parsonage home in Texas.

Pablo, age four and the eldest, Victor, age three, and Rosa, age two, were thrilled with their new home. Not only did they have their own bedroom and a beautiful, fenced backyard, but also a swing and slide, courtesy of the previous occupants. Especially Pablo was excited with their new home, as two of their neighbors also had young children in the same age group, and they quickly became playmates.

Although he was only four years old, Pablo was sure that he wanted to be a minister like his father. Using a soapbox as his pulpit, Pablo would imitate his father as a minister

preaching to his congregation. That playground scenario was repeated many times as he tried to repeat some of his father's sermons. The older kids went along with the game by adding their interpretation of church service by pretending to have a choir, communion, prayer, etc. The younger ones soon lost interest and resumed their own playground games.

Raul Rodriguez, like all ministers of a Methodist Church, was appointed to a different location approximately every four years. Raul's second appointment was in the border city Del Rio, Texas. Three years later, his third appointment was in the West Texas town Colorado City, population approximately 4,000, and where young Pablo, now eleven years in age, received his first paying job.

Walking home from school one day, Pablo was gazing into the window of the local drugstore. The manager, noticing the young boy gazing into his window, walked out in front of this store and approached young Pablo.

"Young man," he asked, "Do you know how to sweep?"

"Yes, Sir," Young Pablo replied.

"Do you know how to mop?"

Wondering why he was being questioned, Pablo hesitated before answering, "Yes, sir."

"Do you know how to wash dishes? And also, what is your name?"

Now sensing he might be asking if he wanted a job, young Pablo enthusiastically answered: "Yes, sir, and my name is Pablo Rodriguez."

"Now I know where I've seen you. You are the new Methodist minister's son, aren't you?"

Once again, he respectively replied. "Yes, Sir."

The owner, Tom Jenkins, was quietly impressed with the young man and especially the politeness and clarity of his answers. "Well, Pablo, I need help, and if you're willing to work I'll give you the job starting tomorrow. I'll need you to work after school four hours a day and eight hours on Saturday and Sunday. Your pay will be four dollars a week, and if you work good, I'll give you a dollar and fifty-cent bonus for Saturday and Sunday."

"Yes, sir, thank you very much, and I sure want the job, but I have a problem working Sunday 'cause I gotta go to church."

The conversation paused for a moment as Mr. Jenkins begin to assess his need for Sunday morning help and still hire the young man who was so painfully honest. "Okay, my young friend, you're hired. I'd like to shake hands with the newest employee of the Lamesa Jenkin's Drugstore. I will look for you after school tomorrow."

Pablo was so excited that his feet barely touched the ground as he could hardly wait to tell the good news to his mother and father. Mr. Jenkins was more than pleased with his new employee and gave even more responsibility as the weeks rolled by. After the fourth month, he trained the young man to make ice cream cones and milkshakes for the customers and even make change in the cash register, quite a step up for a young eleven (near twelve) year old. The customers loved him.

One of Mr. Jenkins' customers was the ticket manager for the local high school sports events and was able to keep Pablo in tickets for most of the high school basketball games and track meets. It became a passion for Pablo and resulted in his activity in those sports later in high school.

Slightly less than two years of employment in Mr. Jenkins drugstore, Pablo had to sadly quit his job as his father was appointed to a new church in Lamesa, Texas. Several attended a farewell party given to the employee by Mr. Jenkins and his customers who had become so attached to the young man. Through donations and a generous contribution from Mr. Jenkins, Pablo was given a fifty-dollar bill for a going away present. Pablo's parents and siblings, along with customers and Mr. and Mrs. Jenkins, shared laughter and tears as the party ended.

Next stop for the Rodriguez family, Lamesa, Texas.

After settling into their new parsonage, it did not take Pablo long to find his next job. One of the new neighbors, having heard the stories about Pablo's job and work ethic in Colorado City, offered him a dollar to mow their lawn and trim their hedges. The good news traveled quickly, and soon Pablo was maintaining lawns for seven residents in the neighborhood. What made it good for him was that, with a flexible schedule, he could continue to participate in the high school sports that he loved. Because he was so good at caring for the yards and his infectious personality, it was a win-win situation for both Pablo and his customers.

At the age of seventeen, graduating fourth in his class with a straight-A average, and still intent on following his father's footsteps into the ministry, he was awarded a scholarship at Texas Wesleyan University in Fort Worth, Texas. He later recalled that leaving home, his mother and father and siblings, was one of the saddest days of his life. However, college would offer a whole new experience, not only of work and study, but meeting many new classmates that would forge lifetime friendships. Also, it did not escape his mind, nor did they go unnoticed, the many beautiful young ladies that were also his classmates. After all, boys do have something on their mind other than sports all the time.

While still in his second year at Texas Wesleyan, Pablo returned to his family's home in Lamesa for his monthly weekend visit. This weekend was also the monthly party sponsored by the church for young singles. Food, music, and games was all that was needed for a great party.

During the break for refreshments Pablo was at the food table grabbing a couple of sandwiches and some chips when he accidentally bumped into a beautiful young lady that was also filling her plate. Pablo and the young lady were attempting to clean up the chips that had scattered on the floor while both were apologizing to each other about the accident. Neither Pablo nor Rita Cortez realized that from that moment together over spilled food resulted in dating that would be the last date they would ever have except with each other.

On almost the same day one year later, and in the same church where they had first met, Pablo Rodriguez and Rita Marie Cortez became Mr. and Mrs. Rodriguez with his father, Reverend Raul Rodriguez, performing the ceremony.

Following a short honeymoon in Ruidosa, New Mexico, the newlyweds begin to realize that his lifelong ambition to follow in his father's footsteps to become a Minister would have to be put on hold. Attending school on a partial scholarship and with only a small added income from part time work, continuing in school was not an option. After much consultation with his father and Rita's parents, they decided to return to their hometown, Lamesa, and temporarily stay with his father and mother until he could obtain a job that would support the two of them.

God works in mysterious ways, because only three days after moving to Lamesa, an ad in the Abilene newspaper stated that a construction company was seeking construction workers for a new Baptist Church in Burson, Texas. The following day Pablo drove to Burson and before the end of the day, following an impressive interview, was a full-time employee with a better than average wage. His good fortune continued as, while still in Burson, he was able to rent a small duplex apartment that could be occupied immediately. The population of Burson was just increased by two.

After a few weeks staying home entering the normal housewife chores, Rita Marie decided she would try to add to their income by working at home. Her first thought what's to attempt to get a job at one of the downtown restaurants as a waitress, but ultimately decided she could make a fair amount of income by, as her mother used to do, taking in ironing and charge for piecework. That would allow her to stay home and still prepare lunch and dinner for her new husband.

Once or twice a week, she would walk several blocks to the new construction site and deliver Pablo's favorite meal, his grandmother's recipe for tacos. Coworkers, all having their lunch nearby, could not help but being envious after smelling the wonderful aroma from the still warm tacos. Eventually, Rita brought a few extra tacos and distributed them among several of the employees. As one thing leads to another, less than a month later, Rita was preparing Taco lunches for several of the construction workers, for a fair, but still profitable, price.

It was only inevitable that the next step would be a small Taco stand in downtown Burson. Nearing the end of the construction project for the new Baptist Church, and after nothing but rave reviews from the city's patrons, and using the savings from his construction job, Pablo and Rita leased a restaurant that had recently closed. After minor remodeling, the first Mexican restaurant in Burson, was open for business.

As previously stated, one good thing often leads to another, after only four very profitable years, a new building, utilizing Mexican architecture, and hiring dozens of employees, was open for business. Pablo and Rita's dream was no longer a dream, but a reality.

Pablo's Mexican Cuisine offered a full Mexican lunch and dinner menu. The most popular item on the menu: Rita Marie's Tacos.

CHAPTER TWENTY-SIX

A Second Conflict with Little Bob Herring

After several years in business, and second only to Gail's Diner as the most popular restaurant in Burson, regular maintenance was a key factor in assuring that the building was always in tip top shape. Roofing, painting, plumbing, electrical, etc. maintenance was on a scheduled plan and was consistently monitored by Pablo personally. The beauty and comfort of Pablo's Mexican Cuisine was a major reason for the popularity of the restaurant by local and nearby town customers.

It was at the scene of what was a regularly scheduled paint job that the second conflict occurred between Pablo and Little Bob Herring. A small local painting contractor, Jeff Fidler, along with his wife Nancy Lee as assistant, was painting the soffit while standing on a scaffold approximately 10 feet above ground while his wife was mixing paint on the ground nearby. It was shortly after lunchtime that little Bob Herring made his appearance at the scaffold.

"What in the hell are you doing here at the restaurant painting when you're supposed to be painting my barn today. You think this damn restaurant is more important than my barn?" The anger and tone of his voice was very violent. Jeff, holding a can of paint in one hand and a brush in the other, turned and attempted to offer an apology.

"I'm so sorry Mr. Herring, but Mr. Rodriguez is hosting a big out of town party tomorrow and asked me if I could finish the painting today. I did not think that you would mind if I were a couple of dates late. I should have called you and asked you if it was okay, and I apologize again we're not doing so."

"Your apology is a bunch of BS and as far as I'm concerned, you could take your paint and your little funky assistant and go to hell. I'll hire another contractor who knows how to keep his appointments."

By now a few employees of the restaurant was taking a break and observing the conversation between the two.

Jeff had just set the paint bucket down on one of the boards of the scaffold as he was still attempting to make apologies to Little Bob. Little Bob, noticing that the young painter had laid the paint can on the scaffold board, grabbed the scaffold frame and to violently shake it attempting to tip the paint can to the ground. This was the moment that a tragic event took place. Reaching for anything to hold onto, Jeff slipped on the paint that had spilled on the scaffold board and fell to the ground below, landing with his back on the previously dislodged paint can.

Fellow employees rushed to the scene of the accident, while some attempted to console his weeping, paint covered, young wife, others were caring for the injured painter. A 911 call was the immediate response of one of the employees.

Little Bob, standing near the scene, only watched the action of the employees of the restaurant for a few moments, and without emotion, turned and walked back toward his car. Pablo, just learning about the accident, met Little Bob face to face as he was rushing to the scene. Neither of the two men exchanged words but the look of hate on Pablo's face was undeniable.

In a low voice, speaking to himself, "Oh God, please, not again."

After examination by doctors in the Emergency Room, it was determined that Jeff had suffered a broken back and a severe head injury. Young Jeff Fidler, after a long convalescence, returned to his occupation as a painter, but never again worked for the Herring Ranch.

Pablo had followed the ambulance to the hospital and remained there until it was clear that young Jeff would eventually recover and be able to return to work. This near-fatal accident only added to Pablo's memory off the previous accidental death of his beloved daughter.

And once again, the blame was squarely on the shoulders of one Mr. Little Bob Herring.

CHAPTER TWENTY-SEVEN

Little Bob and Betty Jean

It was a rainy night in May, slightly cooler than normal, when Betty Jean left her neat little apartment on Eighth Street, and pulled her two-year-old Pontiac Firebird, a graduation gift from her Dad, into the parking lot of Pablo's Mexican Cuisine Restaurant at the corner of Main and Fourteenth. Only a couple of hours after an unusually busy day at the office, and along with the slight chill that filled the air, Tex-Mex food seemed to be the ideal solution to easing her gnawing hunger pains.

Dresses, skirts etc. are not required at work, but being secretary to the "Head Honcho" motivated her to always look her best. Even though she had a large wardrobe of short skirts, snug fitting jeans and revealing blouses, she chose the more conservative things to wear daily to prevent any suspicion or gossip of her relationship with Parker Coburn; that relationship being strictly professional, and she was intent on keeping it that way. Before leaving her apartment, she had slipped into some faded jeans and an ACC Logoed sweatshirt; not the ideal garb to be wearing if you were attempting to attract the opposite sex. However, with those looks, that girl would look good in a gunny sack.

And looking good she was, at least to one Bob Herring Jr., standing just inside the restaurant waiting for a table as she opened the door and entered. After a few seconds to visually explore and soak-in the petite blonde figure standing before him, the expression of pleasant surprise suddenly widened the already present smile on his face.

"Gosh o'mighty, this has to be my lucky day. I was just standing here wishing for a little bit of sunshine on this dreary day and lo and behold, some fairy granted my wish and you appeared."

"And good evening to you, Mr. Herring. How are you?" "Please, Betty Jean; just Bob or Junior; and now that you are here, I feel great. If fact, I feel like Gene Kelley did when he was singing in the rain."

"Well, I don't believe it is raining quite that hard Mr. uh Bob, more like a mist, you know. I have a little trouble picturing you dancing on Main Street in Burson, jumping in and out of puddles with an umbrella and wearing your cowboy hat." "'Nuff said," laughing lightly, "not a good analogy on my feeble attempt at humor. I am assuming that you're alone, and hungry; please be my guest for dinner. The sky is the limit. I have more than adequate funds to completely satisfy your hunger, at least enough to cover a couple of Palo's dinners."

Her first thought was, *No, no, don't go their girl. In fact, don't even think about it. This guy has trouble written all over him.*

Noting her hesitancy, he quickly pleaded, "Aw come on, please. I promise to be the perfect gentlemen. After all, it's just dinner; nothing more than thanks expected in return."

Despite a previous warning to herself, she was intrigued by the prospect of knowing a bit more of the personal side of this handsome young pursuer; and she was hungry. Furthermore, with her cautious financial position, a free dinner with a male companion at Pablo's was becoming an increasingly, attractive offer. Only a brief hesitation on her part before courteously replying, "Yes Bob, I would be happy to join you. Thank you for asking."

The head waiter escorted the couple to a booth by the window with the usual, "Will this table be all right, sir?"

"Okay with you, Betty Jean?"

"Yes, of course. This is very nice, thank you."

"Ramon will be your waiter; he will attend to you shortly. Enjoy your meal." After placing the huge menus on the table, he excused himself.

The dinner experience began a bit on the awkward side as both Bob Jr. and Betty Jean were each trying not to be the aggressive participant in the ensuing conversation. Polite responses, more than needed, were offered freely into the over dinner small talk. After margaritas, two for Junior and one for Betty Jean, the somewhat casual exchange between the two begin to warm up noticeably. Small table talk evolved into bursts of heavy laughter from him and amusing giggles from her. It was obvious to the surrounding diners and restaurant staff that the evening dinner was going quite well for the soon to be "hot new item" in the small west Texas town of Burson.

Almost three hours later, 10:00 p.m. and closing time, Bob Jr. paid the check, along with a generous tip, and escorted his beautiful, young, soon to be his one-and-only-girlfriend, back to her Pontiac Firebird; now parked in an almost empty parking lot.

Smiling graciously, she offered her hand, "Thank you for the delicious dinner. And . . . a lovely evening. I really had a wonderful time."

Responding as he cradled her soft hand into his own, "The pleasure was assuredly all mine, an evening I'll not soon forget."

Impulsively, with right hands still joined, she placed her left hand on his shoulder and pulled him close to her body. After a moment of an affectionate embrace, she reached up and kissed him on the cheek. She turned quickly to open the door to her car but Bob Jr. moving more quickly to reach the door handle, and while acting ever the part of a true gentlemen, opened the door and assisted her inside. She waved as she accelerated away from Pablo's restaurant.

Little Bob Herring stood motionless, gazing at the diminishing taillights until they were completely out of sight. *Betty Jean, you probably don't know this . . . but you're the future Mrs. Bob Herring, Jr. That is as certain as the Sun coming up in the east tomorrow.*

CHAPTER TWENTY-EIGHT

Parker, Betty Jean, and Little Bob: the Triangle

After seventeen months on the job, Betty Jean had grown into a self-assured, confident, respected employee of the Coburn Oil Co. Her fellow employees, as well as Parker himself, were keenly aware of how quickly she had mastered the intricate details of the office, the endless flow of legal documents, and just the everyday run and miscellaneous duties associated with the job. She was loved by all who had any sort of association with her, and she had accumulated dozens of friends in her short tenure in Burson. Just last month, she had been elected secretary of her Sunday school class and had been invited to join the Burson secretary's club, numbering approximately twenty-five secretaries from various business and city government offices.

Her personal social life was not quite the same as in her college days, where a week never passed without a couple of dates, or at least the invitations. The small Texas community was not exactly overrun with unwed or unattached young men her age. She and Parker did have a relationship, of

sorts, but she was constantly on guard not to let it develop into anything too serious. Often, when alone she would admit to herself how much she really cared for him, and the temptation to give in to her impulse to pursue a real romantic relationship. But each time that feeling persisted, the realism of the boss–employee scenario, coupled with the age difference, would smother the physical desire she felt burning inside her body. And thought she deeply admired and respected her superior, the nagging thoughts of it being just another office affair just would not go away. So far, only occasional dinner dates followed by light-hearted conversation parked in front of her apartment, had been the extent of their personal relationship. The physical attraction between the two had graduated into longer good night hugs and more passionate good night kisses, but Parker respectively did not pursue a sexual connection and Betty Jean had offered no physical indication of invitation.

It was a Tuesday morning in early November when Parker entered his office about ten o'clock, two-and-one-half hours later than his normal work time arrival. He had left Betty Jean a note on her desk, before his departure the preceding evening, informing her of his early morning meeting with a potential investor.

Her cheery good morning greeting was returned with equal enthusiasm.

"Morning Bet. How's it going today?" Without waiting for the answer, "Did you get my note from last night saying I'd be late this morning?"

"Great to question one, yes to question two."

Her witty response created a large smile across his well-tanned face as he responded, "Suppose that I got a little hasty with my questions, huh? I should know by now that I can't get ahead of you."

Although he was half-way into the doorway of his personal office, he abruptly returned to her desk and leaned, partially sitting, on her desk facing her chair.

"Hey, I been mulling this over in my mind ever since my meeting with George this morning. He and Clara belong to the local square dance club, and their sponsoring a get acquainted party at the recreation center Thursday night. He assured me that no experience was necessary. It's called a fun party night and the caller teaches a few of the beginning basics. The experienced dancers mix in with the new folks and you start dancing immediately. I have his personal guarantee that we will have the time of our life, and he really twisted my arm for me to grab a date and attend. So . . . I'm thinking; me and you doing the do-si-do. What do think? Oh, and before you answer, he said that the club members bring tons of homemade refreshments. Now I ask you, how could you possibly say no to that?"

"Well, Mr. Smarty Pants, you've no inkling of whom you are messing with. It just so happens that l, having a one-hour credit in physical education specializing in square dancing in college, am practically an expert square dancer. I graciously accept your invitation and I will show you how to Allemande left and right and left grand, and all those other fancy maneuvers." She rose to her feet and executed a twirling motion, exclaiming: "I will even teach you to twirl and promenade."

"Great," was his satisfying reply. "We can get together tomorrow and work out the details."

The parking lot at the Burson Recreation Center was already crowded when Parker wheeled into one of the few vacant parking spots, exited the car and opened the passenger door and assisted Betty Jean out of his Chevrolet Suburban. "Man," he exclaimed, "This must be the place to be tonight. Look at all these cars; seems to me everyone in town is here."

Holding onto his arm as they walked toward the front entrance, she replied, "It doesn't surprise me at all, at our secretary's club luncheon today, a lot of the girls said that they were coming."

Two couples, outfitted in matching colorful square dance attire, greeted them at the door with warm expressions of welcome, handshakes, and hugs. Parker was a bit taken back by the hugs from the two beautifully dressed hostesses, but later was informed that hugging was a long-standing square dance tradition. As they mingled through the assembled crowd, he could not help but being amazed at the number of personal acquaintances in attendance; and in subsequent conversation, how many were already experienced dancers.

Only a few minutes had passed before the rhythmic sound of country hoedown music filled the hall from two large speakers mounted on tripods at each end of the stage. The caller, a well known and respected master of his profession from Abilene, addressed the crowd over his hand-held microphone: "It's square dance time; grab your partner and form one large circle around the floor. Everybody up, no experience necessary, just grab your partner and I'll show you the rest."

Almost one hundred dancers, various ages involved, spent the next few minutes learning the simpler square dance basics, forward and back, circle left and right, do-si-do, right and left grand, right and left-hand stars etc. and proper ways to hold hands and arms while performing the basics. The next phase of introduction was the formation of squares, where dancers randomly broke into groups of four couples. The following twenty minutes or so was actual square dancing to the rhythm of the music and the commands of the caller. Each square was a mix of beginners and experienced dancers, also referred to as "angels." That term is given, universally, to experienced dancers who dance in a square to assist the first timers. The caller ended the first phase of the party by teaching the courtesy involved with the ending of each tip of dancing, a handshake and thank you to each dancer in the square.

Not completely to his surprise, but much more than he expected, Parker was overcome with the pleasure of his first ever Square Dance experience. "Don't ever remember having that much fun in such a short period of time," he loudly expressed his opinion to Betty Jean as he escorted her to the table over-flowing with homemade refreshments.

"I knew you would love it; never had a doubt in my mind."

Parker could not miss the pleasure in her voice and the large smile on her face. This is good, he thought. This feels so right. She is such a joy to be around.

Two more tips of dancing, each teaching session lasting near thirty minutes, was in store for Parker and Betty Jean before the evening ended. Each tip involved the learning of more intricate basics and he mentally patted himself on the back for his expertise in quickly adapting to the calls. The refreshment pauses between the tips of dancing gave Parker time to visit with some of the home-town folks he knew, as well as meeting several new couples with whom he was most pleased to share stories and small talk. JJ Stephens, a single, was dancing with Cynthia, another single, along with Mal Morris and his girlfriend of the month, Beth, were members of the square dance club. Each couple had offered flattering remarks about his dancing ability and encouragement to continue the learning process through a set of weekly lessons beginning in a few weeks. Parker acknowledged his pleasure of this evening and promised that he and Betty Jean would seriously consider the lesson option.

Two hours from the time the caller had picked up the microphone for the opening call, the party was called to a halt with everyone forming a large semi-circle facing the caller and in unison, bowing and then raising hands while expressing vocally, "thank you."

Many, many handshakes, hugs, and expressions of "good night" were exchanged before Parker and Betty Jean made it through the front door and out to Parker's Suburban. After two hours of constant music, dancing and the chatter of friends visiting, the silence inside the Suburban was a welcome change of pace for the two. No words were exchanged as Parker exited the parking lot and turned onto the highway toward Betty Jean's apartment.

She broke the silence, "You surely know that you were pretty dang good out there tonight. I fully expected you to catch on to the complexity of the calls, but you surprised me with how light you are on your feet. You really are a quite good dancer, very smooth and lots of rhythm."

"Thank you. Got that from my Mom, I suppose. When I was a little kid, she used to grab me and make me dance around the kitchen with her, and me, standing on her toes, when a good dance tune came on the radio. Boy, she really loved to dance, but my Dad, he could care less."

Impulsively, she slid across the seat toward him, placed her arm under and around his, and rested her head on his shoulder. He attempted to stay calm and continue driving safely, but his heart was pounding inside his chest at the awareness of her warm body snuggled close to his.

Shortly later Parker parked the Suburban, in what had become a familiar parking spot, under the huge hackberry trees in front of Betty Jean's apartment and switched off the engine and lights. He gently pushed her body, still snuggled on his arm, into a sitting up position and gently gripped both of her hands in both of his own.

"Betty Jean Morrison, I have something to say, and it's very important to me." He lowered his eyes, squeezed her hands more firmly, and took a long period of silence before continuing. Raising his head and making direct eye contact, he followed with, "I, too, will remember the night we sat here after the football game, and your response to my attempt to share my feelings about you. I fully understand your reluctance to pursue this relationship, and the answers you have given me for that reluctance; but if you really understood how much I care for you, then you could understand where I'm coming from now."

She was attempting to come up with some sort of reply, but the words she needed were just not forming in her mind.

Feeling a bit uncomfortable and noticeably stammering, he continued, "I suppose that what I'm trying to ask of you is . . . would you consider pursuing a more serious relationship? I'm not foolish enough to expect you would want to consider marriage or a live-in relationship at this point, but I would hope that a serious courtship might be in order, to see where it leads us."

If Parker was expecting a quick positive response, he was surely disappointed. An eternity of time passed before Betty Jean, visibly shaken by his unexpected proposal, could recover her composure and speak.

"Parker dear, I am at a complete loss for words. There is a part of me that wants to jump into your arms and scream Yes, Yes, Yes. But another part of me is telling me to stop; slow down. I have told you before that above all the people in my life, my Dad is the one I have always leaned on for consul, and Dad has always warned me—do not jump into marriage or a serious relationship on a whim, and particularly, not the first offer. Furthermore, I do have a confession to make to you. You may or may not know, but I have had a few dates with someone else recently, and I do have to admit that I have grown somewhat fond of him. Nothing serious, you understand, but our times together have been enjoyable."

The expression of hurt in his face could not be concealed, and in the instant that she had uttered those words, she was regretting that she had even spoken them.

Oh my God, why did I say that and hurt him so much. How stupid can I be?

"Let me guess, Bob Herring, right?"

"Yes, I assumed you knew."

"No, not really, but I suspected as much. I know how he operates and have overheard a bit of his flirtatious remarks to you at the office. I was hoping that you were smart enough to see through him."

"Parker, I don't want to sound as if I'm defending him, but I've heard all the rumors that circulate about him, and in person he just does not come across that way. As a matter of fact, we've only had a few dinner dates and he has been nothing short of a perfect gentleman. He is hilariously funny to be around, a laugh a minute; but as far as us being anything close to serious, absolutely not! Now, did I detect a little bit of jealously in your remarks?"

Before answering, Parker took a minute to collect his thoughts before carefully choosing his words of response: "Bet, I have no right to judge you or whomever you choose to date. However, I know Bob Herring much better than you do, and I would be remiss if I didn't warn you about him. He has a past that most people do not know, and I urge you to be careful with him. I can assure you that he is trouble with a capital T."

Once again, she found herself at a loss for words, and before she could compose something sensible to say, Parker interrupted, "Bet, having said that about you and Bob, I still stand beside my original pitch to you. I care for you deeply and pray that you will give it serious consideration. Take your time and think about it. I will not push you into anything."

He pulled her close and with a firmer than normal embrace and a good night kiss that lasted longer than normal, suddenly opened his door and without comment, walked to her side of the car to open the door for her. He offered his hand to assist her exit and politely spoke, "Time for goodnight girl, tomorrow's a work-day. See you at the office."

"You've given me a lot to think about, Parker. I wish my Dad were here. I had a lovely evening, and I thank you very much."

She squeezed his hand and walked briskly to her front door.

Chapter Twenty-Nine

A Trip to Las Vegas

Several months passed, and occasional dinner dates gradually involved into frequent fun-filled evenings as the much younger Betty Jean was pursued relentlessly by the handsome eligible, divorced, president of the Herring Enterprises. Having grown up in a family of modest means, the extravagant lifestyle to which she was being treated and the recipient of numerous expensive gifts was proving too much of a temptation to resist. A lavish weekend trip to Las Vegas, first class flight, a five-star hotel suite complete with hot tub and all the amenities, proved to be too much for her personal vow of abstinence of sex before marriage.

All doubts she had harbored about the character of this man, that she had just given herself to, were erased barely twenty-four hours later. Following a romantic dinner on the balcony attached to their suite and overlooking the dazzling kaleidoscope of colored lights overlooking Sin City, Bob Jr. reached into his pocket and retrieved a velvet covered ring box. Leaning across the small dinner table, held her left hand in his left hand, flipped open the box with his right hand

and softly declared: "Betty Jean Morrison, I have made tons of mistakes in my life, and will probably add many more before my time is up. But, having said that, this is not one of them. From the moment I first laid eyes on you in Parker's office, you have been the constant fantasy in my mind. The time we have spent together, since that first dinner at Palos, has only reinforced my feelings for you. My constant dream is that we will spend the rest of our life having fun, enjoying each other's love and companionship, and grow old raising kids and grandkids."

Pausing and struggling to hold back tears, in a still softer voice, "Betty Jean, make me the happiest man in the world tonight. Will you please marry me?"

Shaking almost uncontrollably, she could only drop her head and attempt to hide the torrent of tears rolling from her beautiful blue eyes. Conflicting thoughts were racing through her mind.

What is happening to me? I've heard all the rumors about this man, and most of them not good. He is a spoiled playboy and womanizer, and what about the stories of his shady business dealings? But are they true? He has been nothing but great to me. I've never known him to get out of line, maybe there just rumors, nothing more. He is so sincere, and such a beautiful proposal. Can this really be happening to me?

What she would have sworn to be two or three minutes of time standing still, but in actual time, only thirty seconds or so, was interrupted by a handkerchief being gently placed into her hand by the right hand of her proposer, still squeezing the left.

"Take your time, Honey. I understand this is a lot to throw on you in a short period of time. No need to rush, I'll wait as long as you need." As she blotted her eyes: This may be so wrong, but it feels so, so very right. I know everyone will talk, and my parents will think I'm crazy, but it does feel right . . . and I do love him!

Regaining her composure, she maneuvered her right hand into his left, and extended her left ring finger. Her voice was steady, "Yes, I will marry you Bob, and I love you so very much. You have just made me very, very, happy."

He then slipped the perfectly sized platinum ring onto her finger, a brilliant solitary three-carat diamond, and gently pulled her to her feet. A passionate kiss and hug lingered for minutes. Still arm in arm, her head resting lovingly on his shoulder, they spoke not. Each replaying the previous moments over and over in their mind, they gazed endlessly at the beautiful city below, Las Vegas.

CHAPTER THIRTY

The Day After Vegas

During the return flight Sunday afternoon to DFW airport and the following auto drive to Burson, Betty Jean was trying to keep her emotions in check as she wavered between unbridled excitement and apprehension following her previous night's consent of marriage. Had she made a mistake? Was the overwhelming weekend of romance and extravagant entertaining in Sin City just a case of being too much for a small town girl to handle? How was she going to explain this to her mother and father, the rocks she had leaned on her entire life? She had not even revealed her interest in Little Bob, much less introduced him to them. In fact, most of the conversation she shared with her dad was the reputation of Little Bob in Burson, and that was not a positive one. And even more perplexing was that she had confided to both her mother and father of her interest in Parker, who she held up as shining light of honesty and stability. And still more concerning, how was she to tell Parker? This surely would break his heart.

Totally exhausted from the hours of flying and driving plus the loss of a couple of hours to the change in time zones, she laid her head on Little Bob's shoulder and drifted into an overdue sleep. Arriving at her modest duplex apartment, a goodbye kiss and embrace with her now fiancee and lover was shared with few words exchanged. Little Bob gently lifted her head from his shoulder, "I'll call you at the office tomorrow and we'll set a time to meet and begin discussions on dates, which church, invitation list, honeymoon etc. For now, get some rest. You need it, pretty lady. I love you. Bye, sweetheart."

CHAPTER THIRTY-ONE

The Conversation That Betty Jean Dreaded

The Monday morning that Betty Jean had been dreading, started with the 6:15 a.m. wake-up call from her years-old alarm clock she had had since college. It alternately buzzed from a small decimal tone for a few moments, to another a few seconds later, that would wake the proverbial dead. Today she had to break the news to Parker, and although she had thought about little else the previous few hours, she still had no clue as to what to say or how and when to say it. She did know that she could not dare let him hear it from someone else. It had to be from her personally, and it had to be today. After showering, three changes of clothes before deciding on the proper outfit to wear, a quick breakfast of toast and orange juice, and packing a small lunch bag, she was off to work. She pulled into her parking spot at her usual 8:00 a.m., thirty minutes prior to opening time. She would have coffee brewed and waiting, as always, for Parker when he entered the back door to his office.

The normal arrival time for Parker, 8:15 a.m., came and went. Then It was 8:45 a.m., then 9:00 a.m. and not even the courtesy phone call to Betty Jean informing her he was going to be late. Betty Jean paced the floor with busy work, several times glancing out the window overlooking the employee parking hoping to see Parker's Suburban pulling into the lot.

Paul Hicks, the geologist, exited his office heading for the kitchen area, "Like me to freshen up your coffee while I'm pouring Bet?"

"Thanks anyway Paul, but I've just about had my fix for the morning." Hesitating momentarily, she tried to hide the anxiety in her voice, "Guess our boss man must have dropped off at Gail's for a real breakfast, must not have been in the mood for my-to-die-for java today."

Paul took a sip from his cup before exclaiming, "Wow, that is some hot, but good. Nah, just forgot to tell you. He called me a bit earlier asking about the latest report we ran on the Driscoll lease. He mentioned that he wasn't feeling all that well and would come in a bit later today. Said just tell everyone to hold down the fort 'till he feels better." Gingerly cradling his smoking coffee cup, he slowly walked back to his office without spilling a drop.

Quarter-hours became half-hours and half-hours became hours as Betty Jean was becoming increasingly aware that her chances of being the first to tell Parker about her trip to Las Vegas with Little Bob were slipping from slim to none. Near 1:00 p.m., not hungry but forcing down small bites of a peanut-butter-and-banana sandwich she had hastily thrown together before rushing from home that morning, she recognized the familiar chugging sound of Parker's diesel pickup. She quickly disposed of the half-eaten sandwich in the nearby waste basket and pretended to being diligently at work.

Raising her head slightly and turning toward the approaching Parker she smiled and good naturally asked, "See you're driving your pickup today, must be going out to the new lease. And, too much of Palo's enchiladas and salsa got your stomach complaining?"

Without pausing, Parker continued to walk to his office as if he were hurrying to avoid all conversation, even small talk. "Yes Bet, I may check out the new lease later, but feeling bad, can't blame it on Palo this time. Just one of those days. In other words, I've had better ones."

Parker remained mostly isolated in his office that afternoon, only once coming out just long enough to carry a handful of papers to Paul's office, and then returning and only nodding at Betty Jean as he returned.

"Oh, dear God, he knows. He's got to know. How can I ever explain this to him?"

Normal closing time at Parker Oil and Gas was 5:00 p.m., but Betty Jean often worked late, normally several more minutes finishing up last minute details etc. and particularly for the personal interaction with her boss and best friend, Parker Coburn. But today was significantly different and she knew she had to make her move right now.

She quickly took a glance into her ever-present pocket mirror for a last-minute hair and makeup checkup, and then strode quickly to the open door of Parker's adjacent office. She paused, and simultaneously knocked a couple of taps and cheerfully asked, "Got a minute Parker?"

Parker lowered some legal papers he pretended to be studying, removed his reading glasses, and leaned back in his chair responded, "Sure, Bet, always got time for you. Have a seat. What's on your mind?"

Small beads of moisture begin to form in her eyes as she, in a very subdued voice, begin to speak. "Parker, when I asked you for the day off Friday for personal issues I, uh, did not reveal to you my plans for the weekend. I presumed you would ask, but knowing what a gentleman you are, I should have known that you probably already knew and was just too nice to inquire."

"Don't quite know what to say, but . . . "

She quickly interrupted his attempted reply, "Please, Parker, let me get this off my chest. I know that you love me, and you have treated me with such respect. I cherish very much the many, many good times we've shared. I, too, love you Parker. I also know that my dad and mother love you and really wanted it to work out for us. Daddy would be in the proverbial hog's heaven with you, being the honest Christian man that you are, as a son-in-law."

"Woah, Bet, that's laying it on a little thick, don't you think?"

"Please, please, Parker! Let me finish. This is really hard for me."

By now what earlier had been only a slight number of tears appearing in her eyes, were swelling into large tears sliding down her cheeks, as it were raindrops on an outside window in a rainstorm. She was attempting to empty her soul to the man that she, only three months ago, had seriously considered accepting his offer to become Mrs. Parker Coburn. Now crying uncontrollably, she was frantically reaching for a tissue when Parker shoved the box, on his desk, into her searching hands.

"Easy, Bet, it's okay," he spoke with such compassion. "After all, this is a small town, and it is really hard to keep a secret with all these busy-bodies we have that thrive on the local gossip. Matter of fact, I've known for some time that my chances with you had pretty much gone out the window. You know, early on, I told you about my concern for the age difference; great for me, but not so much for you. And once you begin to date Little Bob, someone much more compatible in age, and with that handsome look and personality to boot, I pretty well knew my days were numbered."

She tried to get back into her explanation of the past weekend's events, but Parker insisted, "Hold on Honey, you had your turn. Now it's mine. "I care for you so very, very much, Bet. And in all honesty, would give most anything I own to have you as my wife for the rest of my life. But I am a realist, and if I am to be true to myself, not my selfish self, I probably am not young enough to assure you the kind of enduring lifetime commitment you so richly deserve."

Now more composed, she again entered the conversation, "There is one thing I did not get to say, Parker, and it is the hardest part of the story." She noticeably stammered, "Little Bob proposed, and I accepted. The truth is, I never saw it coming. It was like a bolt out of the blue. I remember my dad always telling me: Never consider marriage seriously until, one day, love will hit you like a ton of bricks; and then you will know that he is the one. And so, Parker, although I did and do love you, I never felt the bricks until Little Bob proposed. And for hurting you, and I know that I did, I will forever be regretful."

Parker wheeled his office chair toward the window for a minute, obviously searching for the proper reply to the news that just broke his heart. He slowly turned back to face this young employee, reconstructed his thoughts, and in a very emotional voice: "Bet, and I never saw that coming, if it could not be as the lucky one, I really wish it had not been him. You surely know the problems I have had with him, as well as half of the people in this town. I know this sounds like sour grapes on my part, but Honey, I know so much more about him than you do."

"I know all of the rumors, Parker, but I just can't help but think that most of it is greatly exaggerated. He has sworn to me that practically all the things he has been accused of are false and have never been proven in court. He did tell me about Palo's daughter and the abortion that turned out badly; and that he would regret it for the rest of his life."

"Bet, please, for God's sake, just think rationally, not out of emotion."

"But don't you see, people can change. He even explained about Mal's mother's accident. He swore that he had too much to drink and his girlfriend insisted that she drive. He explained the reason he bought her a new car afterwards so that she could get over her guilt and get on with her life. The local folks all thought it was a payoff, but it wasn't."

The room grew extremely silent as both, as two boxers between rounds, paused as if their will to fight had eroded, their energy expended.

Parker broke the silence, "I'll not say anything else negative. I do owe you an apology, and I am really, really sorry for acting the way that I did. I should be congratulating you instead of making disparaging remarks. It's sort of like I was raining on your parade."

"No, you should not apologize. You said your piece and had the right to do so. Parker Coburn, you are remarkable, and you will always hold a special place in my heart. I may someday regret my decision, but for now, I am positive it was the correct one."

"One last thing Betty Jean, and I'll say no more. Young Mr. Herring has a sometimes out of control temper and bad things, you don't know about, have happened. If he ever gets physical and hurts you, I promise that he will have to answer to me. You may not want me to, but that is a promise that I will keep."

Betty Jean arose from her chair, extended her hand, and quietly asked, "Friends?"

With both hands on the front of his desk, he pushed himself to his feet, accepted her extended hand into his own, forced a smile, and slowly replied, "Friends."

She returned to her desk, gathered her purse and personal items, and slowly walked to her car in the rear lot. Climbing beneath the wheel, the engine jumped to life as she turned the ignition to start. She grabbed a tissue for her tear-filled eyes, then slowly drove out of the parking lot and headed toward her small duplex only a few blocks away.

Her mind was like a small whirlwind bouncing from one thought to another as she tried to recap the events of the last hour. Finally, she left the meeting with Parker behind and quietly spoke to herself, "One down, one to go." So fearful of impending disappointment, the one to go was to be her mother and father. They were the ones she was most dreading to tell.

CHAPTER THIRTY-TWO

Next up, Mom and Dad

The following day was surprisingly uneventful with no mention of the previous evening's discourse. Parker and Betty Jean worked together as if nothing had changed. The interaction dialogue between her fellow workers seemed that no one was aware of the already wildfire-like spreading gossip regarding her and Little Bob's Las Vegas weekend getaway. Although she, never one to settle for a routine forty-hour week, had previously decided that this was the day to leave at the accustomed closing time with the clear intent of clearing her second obstacle, a visit with Mom and Dad.

"Parker, provided that you don't need me for anything else today, I'm leaving now; got a few things to do."

"That's fine, Bet. I'll lock up when I leave. Have a good time."

She guided her well travel-tested Pontiac out of the lot and headed south toward her hometown, Eastland, Texas. Although her mind was clogged with apprehension, fearful as to how her parents would react to the what had to be surprising, news, she nervously tapped her fingers on the steering wheel as she traveled through minimal traffic on the black asphalt West Texas highway. Her apprehension and fear slowly evolved into a feeling of peace and solitude. She was aware of their love for her and their always willingness to listen, understand and forgive.

Slightly less than two hours later, she was in her mom and dad's arms, showered with hugs and kisses. The discussion came later, after dinner. The breaking of the news, she had so dreaded to reveal, was met with little dissent. The unwavering support to their only child was undeniable.

She was not disappointed.

After helping her mom with the dishes and clean up, she sought a brief conversation with her Father regarding her still respectful feelings of Parker. She wanted his advice as to how she should handle the situation. After lowering his head and taking a few minutes to consider her request, he offered what he thought to be the best way for her to proceed. He advised her to immediately offer her resignation, but to continue to work until a competent replacement could be hired. Also, out of respect for Parker, she should stay on the job a reasonable length of time to help train his new secretary.

Relieved, she knew that her dad always offered her good advice, she entered her old bedroom for a good night's sleep.

Her wonderful, loving, mom, had already turned-down her bed, and placed a glass of water on the adjoining night table.

CHAPTER THIRTY-THREE

Planning the Wedding

Fully aware of the tedious situation that he found himself in between his new fiancée and her employer, a fragile one at best, Little Bob refrained from calling Betty Jean at work. However, he called her each evening, almost to the minute, that she arrived home. He was respectful of her desire for a church wedding, although he was hopeful that they could be married in his father's church, the largest sanctuary in Burson, the First Baptist Church. He envisioned a large number on the visitation list, a full orchestra and a catered dinner reception at the Burson Country Club following the service.

Completely aware of the elaborate planning that he had outlined to her so enthusiastically, she was almost inclined to not burst his bubble. However, a pretentious wedding and a spare-no-expense reception with dozens or maybe even a hundred or so guests, was not the wedding she had always dreamed of having. Reluctantly, after several days of mostly listening to his exclusive planning, she intervened with her own ideas. Those ideas were considerably in contrast to what had been previously discussed, primarily all Little Bob's plan.

She expressed her gratitude for his vast amount of work that he has so obviously spent on so many details of their upcoming nuptials. However, she would much prefer a smaller, much smaller, service in the church that she grew up in, and that her parents were still active members of, the Eastland United Methodist Church. A small invitation list of close friends and family, her long time and still active minister officiating, and a reception in the Church Fellowship Hall immediately following the wedding service, would be her strong preference. In other words, this would be the wedding of her dreams.

After the initial shock about her not wanting the wedding he was sure that she would love, he realized the passionate desire that she had expressed for the smaller, more familiar church with hometown friends as guests, wedding in Eastland.

"Sweetheart, I love you so much that I'll marry you under the mesquite tree, if they have one, in your daddy's backyard. You just do the planning, and I will get out of your way. Just don't set the date too far away, okay? If you need any help, just let me know. I do have a few connections in Eastland myself, you know."

She literally jumped to her feet, wrapped both arms around his neck, and followed with a lingering, passionate kiss.

"I love you I love you . . . and go home. I'm still a working girl, you know, and I got to get up early. Now get out of here and go . . . go . . . go."

"I got the hint . . . I'm gone. Call you tomorrow."

Chapter Thirty-Four

Betty Jean Reveals the Good News

Slightly less than sixteen months after their wedding in nearby Eastland, Betty Jean broke the good news to her husband at the dinner table. She had prepared his favorite meal of homemade meatloaf with gravy, corn on the cob and scalloped potatoes. She purposefully filled the evening conversation with trivial news about her shopping trip to the local JC Penney store and having a burger and fries at the Dairy Queen. Then to make the evening more special, demonstrating her culinary skills, she rose to her feet and retrieved a still warm freshly baked Pecan pie from the oven.

"My God, Honey, what did you do, wreck the car or something? Is this a make-up offering, or did you do something even worse? Is this like . . . like a peace offering?"

"No, my darling husband, would you like to try again?" "Traffic ticket?" he inquired, with a pretentious frown of disgust.

"Not getting any warmer," she chuckled.

Throwing up both hands in the air, "I give up, it must be your mother and dad are coming to visit and you are just wanting to test your cooking prowess on me."

Smilingly proudly, she leaned over, kissed him on the cheek, and whispered, "Hi Daddy!!!"

Even the smartest people in some fields of endeavor are often the dumbest in others. Hence the puzzled look on Little Bob's face as he tried to make sense out of what seemed to him to be a stupid remark for his young wife to make. He sat there without speaking, just thinking, when she interrupted his silence.

Reaching over and taking his hand in hers, she guided it, palm up, and gently started rubbing it in a circular motion over her stomach.

"Meet your new son or daughter, Mr. Herring. What do you think, boy or girl?"

The expression on his face went from like the proverbial "Night to Day," from a stunned look of inquisition to that of complete joyful surprise.

"You are kidding me, right . . . kidding me? Say you are not kidding me. Oh my God, you are not kidding me."

In his excitement while jumping to his feet, he overturned his dinette chair and almost fell to the floor. He grabbed her into his arms and was frantically kissing her again and again, pausing only long enough to loudly proclaim, "I'm going to be a father . . . and a dang good one also."

The party of only two's celebration continued long into the night. There were all sorts of plans for their future discussed, that would be subsequently re-discussed over and over in the following weeks. At exactly seven months and two days later, the newest addition to the Herring family arrived at promptly 8:30 a.m. at the Burson General Hospital. A six-pound seven-ounce baby girl was delivered without any undue complications to either the mother or daughter, and a proud papa was there to witness the entire precious moment.

One year and six months later, another beautiful baby girl, and in the same delivery room, made her presence known to the world. Brenda Kaye, joining big sister Emily Jean, would become the last additions to the Little Bob and Betty Jean Herring family.

Chapter Thirty-Five

Mr. and Mrs. Bob Herring Jr, 1972-1980

Like most new married couples, Little Bob, and Betty Jean, madly in love, spent many happy hours together. Movies, the local theater, country music festivals, local sports, picnics on the ranch, or you name it, anything was alright if they were together. The birth of their two children was a blessing and their love and care for the young girls was a given. However, after the birth of their second daughter, the love between the two begins to deteriorate.

Little Bob's addiction to alcohol, that he had kept in moderation during the early years of their marriage, was now becoming a problem. Small disagreements, that during the first years was just a slight difference of opinion, now had reached the "in your face" kind of arguments that became louder and physical. Betty Jean's less interest in sex, after the birth of her second daughter, was one of the major problems in their marriage. Betty Jean's explanation to her husband was that after taking care of her daughters all day, as all mothers do, was so tiring that she just wanted to go to bed and get a good night's sleep. She also told him that she still was in love with him and hoped that he could understand and respect her feelings. Also, she asked him to please cut down on the amount of alcohol that he was consuming as it was quickly becoming a problem. And like most alcoholics, he denied her accusation.

Due to his addiction, everyday business transactions that were at one time routine, now became obstacles too complex to overcome. Adding to his frustration was the almost daily legal charges that required his legal team to defend. It was as if each one of the Friday Five, for one reason or another, was weekly reporting him to the Sheriff, and the only thing that relieved his emotional pain was more and more drinking.

As an old saying goes, "you always hurt the one you love," was a very real experience for his wife Betty Jean. The once slightly physical arguments evolved into excessive physical attacks on his beautiful wife. Most of her injuries, bruises from being kicked and punched, she tried to conceal with makeup or just by staying home and out of sight until they were healed. The times that required medical attention was explained as falling because of clumsiness or carelessness around the horses in the corral. Although her friends knew better, she would not admit to any violent attacks from, or place any blame on, her husband.

That was a secret that she would never reveal, one that she would carry to her grave.

Chapter Thirty-Six

A Meeting of the Friday Five

On an early Friday in March 1980, Gail's Diner was in full swing on as Bull Bullock and the rest of the Friday Five were enjoying the delicious home cooking and the good-natured ribbing and jokes between the long-time friends. Bull, after spreading a heaping pad of whipped butter on the remaining half of the "melt in your mouth" tasty rolls before consuming the entire portion in one large bite, wiped his mouth and emptied his ice-tea glass before speaking, "Would you look at that? Boy, that chaps my you know what every time I see that SOB still free on the street. He ought to be so far back in a Huntsville six by twelve suite that they would have to Pony Express his mail—if he were lucky enough to ever get any!"

The cause of anger was in response to Bull having observed Little Bob Herring driving past the Diner in his new dark green Silverado.

"Ditto on that, Bull. Even that's too good for him as far as I concerned."

Mal Morris, with his eyes squinting for clarity, was intently following the pickup as it was pulling out of sight.

JJ Stephens, raising his half-filled tea glass, "Think I'll just propose a little toast." Parker and Palo joined the toast as the other two, almost in unison, raised their glasses in genuine consent. JJ continued, "To Bob Herring Jr.: may his soul rot in the eternity of hell, and sooner rather than later." The toast was consummated by the distinct clicking of glass, and the sound of heavy swallowing that followed.

The scorn and contempt verified by the spoken toast was rightfully deserved, at least in their own mind, according to each member of the Friday Five. Every one of the five present had been victimized by Bob Jr. on more than one financial enterprise, promoted by the smooth-talking promoter.

Efforts to bring justice to the accused, for fraud, theft, and swindling, had twice previously failed. TV and newspaper accounts of the lengthy trials were prominent in their coverage. Special reporters were assigned full-time to follow the trials and research the "behind the scenes" stories.

With the Herring fortune and his father's trust and political clout behind him, both trials had ended in a mistrial via lack of unanimous jury approval. The high-priced legal team from Austin, engaged by Bob Herring Sr., was far too much for the local district attorney with limited experience and resources, to overcome. He was simply overmatched.

Mal Morris again, "Seriously, you know, somebody's going to take him out some day. He's just hurt too many decent people and got way too many enemies. One thing for sure, and as sinful as it sounds, somebody needs to."

The others, either with nods or verbal responses, echoed their agreement.

That is, all but one. Parker Coburn, the person who had taken the biggest financial hit of all, was conspicuously silent. He also was the one most personally involved with Bob Jr. through their joint ownership of a half-dozen producing wells. It also was not without the knowledge of all parties present, that a few years earlier, both men were vying for the affection of one beautiful young lady, Betty Jean Morrison. That love drama had been unfolding since the time of her tenure at Parker Coburn Oil & Gas Company.

The lust for further discussion of Little Bob's future diminished as Bull rose to his feet, a signal from their leader, and pronounced, "Let's save it for another day, boys. Enjoyed the dinner and confab. 'Till next time!"

The usual parting phrases, "See you 'round, so-long guys, *Adios Amigos,*" flowed from one ear to the other. This week's meeting of the Friday Five had adjourned.

Chapter Thirty-Seven

Who is Little Bob? Continued

Crushed with guilt and remorse, embarrassed to be with school friends, Little Bob attempted to drown his sorrow by working long hours in his father's business. Although his mother and father were heartbroken to see the extent of their son's problems, they were most helpless in trying to make him feel better and return to his normal personality. He was determined to learn every aspect of the business and prove to his parents that he was worthy of being their son and future heir. Because of the mistake of his young life that had occurred in Lubbock, his desire to attend Texas Tech College was no longer in his plans. It goes without saying, his parents had a different plan in mind, college for their son was a must.

After research and discussion with each other, he agreed to attend Northwest Texas Junior College in nearby Graham Texas. Only approximately an hour's drive from home he would not stay on campus but commute on school days. His decision was to pursue a business degree, and often, depending on class hours, could be home in time to see how his classes might apply to his father's business.

Two years later with a modified business degree and the honor of finishing in the top ten of his class, Little Bob returned home to continue his plan of earning his father's trust and becoming president in his family business.

Late one evening while still at work little Bob received a phone call from one of his classmates in junior college. Melinda Martin, a beautiful blonde cheerleader who lived in Graham, asked him how things had gone with him since graduation.

He responded explaining the many hours he was spending learning his father's business anticipating that soon he would be taking over as company president.

She offered her congratulations and added small talk about herself and uncertain plans for her future. Also, she had hoped to meet him some time and reminisce their good old college days.

Surprised that she was contacting him as they had only dated once in college, and she did not seem to be overjoyed with the evening, just sort of a ho-hum date. After his initial negative thinking about her and their one and only date, a second thought was that it had been a long time since he had been with a young member of the opposite sex. A date with Melinda might be just the frosting on the cake that he needed.

Twenty-five minutes later, he asked if she would be interested in a dinner date and maybe a movie afterwards. After replying that it would be her pleasure to accept his invitation, both agreed on the following Friday as a date, and that he would pick her up at six o'clock and she would choose the restaurant.

Polite goodbyes were exchanged. Little Bob held the receiver for a few moments before hanging it up. *More and more I'm thinking this date will be the frosting on the cake.*

At six o'clock sharp little Bob pulled into the driveway of the modest home where Melinda still lived with her parents. Melinda, obviously watching for her date to arrive, was halfway down the sidewalk before he could even open the car door. He quickly walked toward her and escorted her to the passenger side of the car, and like a real gentleman, opened the door and helped her into the passenger seat.

The dinner they shared, at one of the nicer restaurants in Graham, was enjoyed by both as they exchanged stories from their previous college days with lots of alternating giggles and laughter. The time spent at the restaurant far exceeded what they both had expected and was much too late to attend a movie. Driving aimlessly around town, searching for a place to maybe park and continue the conversation, she directed him to a nearby park where under a star-filled sky highlighted by a much larger than normal moon, the conversation resumed.

Nearing eleven o'clock, hand holding evolved into hugs, and hugs evolved into kissing and less talking. Sensing it was getting late and he did not want her parents to be wondering what was happening on their first date, he politely echoed his reason for ending the first date and drove her back to her home.

A decision for a second date was a given, followed by a goodnight kiss at the door and a brisk walk back to his car. Little Bob quickly began his journey back home, feeling that this might just be the one. Also, the first date was certainly the frosting on the cake, and maybe, just maybe the next date might include the ice cream that goes with the cake.

Only four months after their first date, Bob Herring Jr. and Melinda Martin were married by a Justice of the Peace in Breckenridge, Texas. Revealing that she might be pregnant, Little Bob was not about to make the same mistake that he had made in Lubbock three years earlier.

Lake Murray Lodge in southern Oklahoma was the chosen site to celebrate their honeymoon. Both newlyweds had previously visited the lodge, as younger children, with their parents. The honeymoon suite along with better than average lodge meals and a boat outing on the beautiful Lake Murray contributed to a short, but wonderful, two days together.

The Herring ranch house, a large two-story house measuring near 6,000 square feet set on one of the higher elevations of the property, had been home to the Herring family for the past 28 years. The east wing had two large bedrooms with a nice bathroom and closets downstairs. The upstairs bedroom with an extra-large bathroom and walk-in closet was considered to be the master bedroom. Both the upstairs and downstairs bedrooms had an adjoining den with a small bar and television. The upstairs bedroom also had a nice-sized balcony overlooking hundreds of acres of the Herring Ranch. The east wing master bedroom had been little Bob's room since starting his senior year in high school, but now there is a new occupant, moving in immediately, Mrs. Bob Herring.

Bob Sr. and Lillian had both been introduced to Melinda by their son when he invited his parents to join them for dinner at Palo's restaurant in one of their early dates. Caught off guard by their rush to be married and then immediately joining the Herring household, both parents were gracious and welcomed her into the family with hugs and smiles. All her personal items that she wanted to be moved into her new home could be picked by one of their ranch hands with a truck at her desired date. Melinda Martin Herring was now officially the newest member of the Herring family.

Six weeks later and after Bob Sr. had been analyzing the positive progress Little Bob had achieved in his knowledge of the company, he decided the time was ripe to inform his son of his retirement plan. The plan was simple. He would immediately initiate the paperwork that would officially make little Bob the new president of the family business. He and Lillian had built a smaller house on the ranch property overlooking a small lake with a picturesque view. The smaller house would require much less work and their longtime housekeeper, Joni, would only be needed once a week. She would continue to work at the big house the remaining four days of the week, thus giving the new Mrs. Bob Herring Jr. the help required to upkeep the larger house.

The following day Bob Sr. called Bob Jr. into his office to reveal his decision. Little Bob would be promoted the president of the Herring Ranch effective immediately. Paperwork required would be initiated this day. It is now official, Little Bob is in charge. Also, the elder Herring family retirement plan is official.

Close to six weeks after their marriage, Melinda informed Little Bob of the good news that he had prayed for was granted. A visit to her doctor revealed that she was not pregnant. The jubilant husband would no longer have to burden the embarrassment surrounding the hasty wedding. Also, the town gossips would not need an explanation. What he didn't know, Melinda already knew what the test would reveal.

Unlike major cities where there is usually a definite divide between the extremely rich and the average income residents, Burson social membership was limited to primarily the country club members with occasional programs featuring outside speakers or dinner dances. Club members had tee time priority for the golf course but often members as well as walk-ons were paired together.

Melinda Herring wasted no time in advancing her agenda to become the latest Burson socialite. Frequent visits to the country club allowed her the opportunity to introduce herself to small and large groups of members, emphasizing the Herring name. Although she could only become a big fish in a small pond, she was well on her way to reaching her goal.

Meanwhile, back at the ranch, Bob Jr. was spending more and more hours trying to increase the company profits in an economy that was tail spinning and not having the success that he had hoped to achieve. Also, after several months, the marriage between he and Melinda began to unravel. Not happy with Melinda's constant involvement with the country clubbers and her spending less and less time at home, he began to suspect a proverbial "fly in the ointment." It just might be that the reason she had initiated the phone call that brought them together was the fact that she had previously heard that he soon would become the president of the family business. She probably did love him, but her primary goal was to become a socialite celebrity.

Barely over twenty-three years of age, and after slightly over two years of a tumultuous marriage, Little Bob and his want-to-be-celebrity wife were divorced. Two years of boomeranging insults and accusations had provided the local newspaper with more than needed salacious material for newsprint. Even the paid gossip columnist required little research to fill her weekly column, other than the Herring brawl. Eventually, well paid opposing lawyers persuaded both plaintiff and defendant to agree on an out of court settlement. Financial terms were sealed, but rumors abounded that Little Bob took a financial kicking. Fortunately, Bob Sr., after retiring quite handsomely, although not happy with the settlement, could easily afford to help his son with the several hundred thousand dollars thought to be the final award to the defendant.

Despondent and lonely, with the stress of the nasty divorce proceedings between himself and first wife Melanie, he was constantly drifting into and out of a state of depression. Having turned to alcohol, the proverbial crutch, much of his enthusiasm for work and business was all but lost. Without quality leadership and coupled with a failing economy, the financially strong Herring Enterprises began a rapid down-hill spiral. Losses were mounting daily and Bob Jr., as company president was the one being held accountable. Bob Sr. had not taken the action to "right the ship" but just keep a cautious eye on the developments. However, he was keenly aware of his only son's excessive drinking habits and had personally cautioned him about his increasing addiction to the devil's cocktail. Hoping that the younger Herring would work his way out his troubles and the company fortunes would turn around, the elder Herring had remained patient.

As is the case with all alcoholics, they almost unanimously deny the fact that they have a problem. Little Bob was not an exception to that fact. Bob Herring Sr. reluctantly decided that he must take action to save his son. This meeting with his son was one that of a loving father having to inform his son that there were only two options to choose from, register in a facility that treats alcoholism, or give up his job as manager of the Herring estate. Facing the fact that he really had no choice, Little Bob agreed to enroll in an institute in Fort Worth, Texas. The family minister made the arrangements and Little Bob was enrolled the following Monday.

After only one week and two days later, Little Bob's addiction got the better of him and he left the program and went on a drinking spree for the next three or four days. Sitting under a bridge with other homeless people, he was startled to see his father and mother park and approach him. Once inside the car, he began to openly cry and beg for their forgiveness. The next few minutes was that of both sadness and jubilation. The fear of being lost and alone was over. The family was back together.

Two weeks of rest, good home cooking and no stress was the treatment he so badly needed, and his recovery was imminent. The following week he eagerly agreed to return to the Alcohol Institute in Fort Worth that was willing to give him a second chance. Six weeks later he was released and was greeted with open arms by his jubilant parents. He was back on the job, but many business problems still existed, and they needed to be addressed immediately.

With his company in the financial doldrums, and his personal life in total disarray, Little Bob was desperate to get both his life and the company turned around. Money and love were what he needed, and both were becoming more difficult to acquire. It seemed the harder he tried, the bigger the roadblocks became. Desperate times sometimes lead to desperate measures, and Little Bob was not above a little fudging with law and ethics to get his house back in order. Schemes and plans circulated through his mind non-stop, and at first his only motive was to regain some financial clout, by whatever means, legal or not, and make restitution when things got better. But as is often the case in fraud and swindle cases, the further you go the easier it becomes to continue. Bob Jr. was headed down a path of no return.

The first scheme implemented was the illegal transfer of oil, via one of Bob's truckers, from storage tanks owned jointly with Parker, to a nearby storage facility that he solely owned. The same employee, paid accordingly for his service and keeping his mouth shut, was also responsible for juggling the gauging reports to reflect lesser production in the jointly owned wells; and more into the one owned by Little Bob.

The adrenaline rush resulting from the success of his transfer scheme only fueled more and more ideas of fraud and swindle. As a lease salesman, or in the trade sometimes referred to as lease hounds, Bob Jr. had been reasonably successful in his apprentice years with his father's company. During that time, a few of the independent oil and gas companies had been purchasing existing leases with the idea of deeper re-drilling in order to reach more productive pay zones. Other properties not yet under lease were becoming targets for exploration to the new zones. Most traditional leases offered the landowner twelve and one-half percent royalty, or over-ride, with the leasing company keeping the remaining eighty-seven-and-one-half percent. The leasing company was to cover drilling and the completion costs, a turn-key offer to the landowner. In turn, the leasing company would then offer eighty percent to potential investors, usually in packages known as prospectuses, as low as two-and-one-half percentages, and up to whatever percentage the investor was willing to purchase.

The plan, although devious, was simple in Little Bob's mind. If the well had proven to be a dry hole, or not productive enough to return the investment, the well would be plugged. Afterwards, no further accounting to the oil and gas commission would be required. And with the Herring Company doing the drilling, a dry hole was assured. By manipulating the accounting, he could easily sell up to one hundred twenty or more percent in a single investment to unsuspecting clients, and no one would be the wiser.

Not only did the plan work, but it worked well. The unaccounted percentages, worth several thousand dollars, went directly into several different personal bank accounts, but not one in his hometown bank.

Greed overrode the original intentions of, once he had gotten back on his financial feet, complete restitution to the defrauded investors; some of whom were friends and neighbors who had put their complete trust into the hometown family-owned Herring Enterprises. Unable to accept the fact that he was guilty of anything morally wrong, and despite his strong Christian up-bringing, he drove full speed ahead down the path of eventual self-destruction. Each successful scheme served only to boost his confidence that he would never be caught; and now he was back on top. And back on top, come hell-or-high-water, he was determined to stay.

CHAPTER THIRTY-EIGHT

The Meeting with the Poker Draw

The parking lot of the Church of Christ, located at Eighth Street and Magnolia Avenue, filled quickly on this cold dreary Friday morning in February of 1980. Even with pew seating for two-hundred-fifty and the addition of folding chairs, many mourners were forced to stand due to the overflowing crowd. Family members joined friends, fellow church members, neighbors, and many in the assembled group of only casual acquaintance, in paying their mutual respect to the recently deceased Joe and Bernice Benson.

Joe and Bernice, in their upper seventies and life-long residents of Burson, were loved and respected by all who knew them personally. Their reputation within the community was unequaled. Only the preceding Wednesday a neighbor, concerned after no response to her telephone calls, had discovered the bodies of the elderly couple in their home, apparently the result of a pre-agreed murder–suicide pact. A jointly signed note had explained their reasons and had been deemed authentic by the investigating law enforcement office.

After a beautiful and very moving service, the caravan of cars, making up the funeral procession, wound its way one and one half-mile west to the Memorial Garden Cemetery. The huge group huddled closely to the grave site, seeking protection from the biting north wind, for the short final service. Final condolences and tearful exchanges of compassion were offered to the family members as the remaining mourners quietly took their leave. No one left the service without feeling a deep sense of sadness for the loss of two ordinary, but incredible special people.

"Damn it, it's just not right . . . for anybody, especially someone like Joe and Bernice, just not right." Bob Bullock was grimacing with obvious pain and disgust as his face twisted into a snarl. It was shortly before twelve noon and each one of the Friday Five had arrived and were seated at their usual table at Gail's Diner. All five had attended the service and had come directly to the diner following the service. Each of the wives of the Five had previously obligated themselves to help serve dinner at the Benson family home for the immediate family and friends. The guys, with Bob's urging, had decided to proceed with their weekly routine.

JJ responded, "I'll double down on that. As far as I'm concerned, something has to be done about that SOB; and pretty dang quick."

No words were spoken, only mumbling and nods of agreement, but everyone knew exactly who JJ was referring to as "that SOB."

Leaning forward and lowering his voice, Bullock began, "Listen up Boys, I have a plan. I honestly don't know if I have the stomach for this, or even if any of you do, but I've been thinking about this long and hard."

Mal Morris also in a low voice, "Cut to the chase, Bob, let's hear it."

"Okay, here's the deal. We all know Bob Jr. didn't pull the trigger, but he might as well have. And more or less, same thing happened to Jessie Henley eight months ago. Only thing different was he didn't have time to shoot himself, the heart attack from stress got him first. And it wouldn't surprise me in the least that poor old Johnny Copland didn't also die from stress, after he lost everything he had saved for forty years. And all of it because of those swindling deals that silver tongued devil sold to those defenseless good folks."

Mal with urgency in his voice, "Come on Bob, we all know that. Like we've said a gillion times, those high-priced lawyers out of Austin are gonna keep him out of jail and on the street, so, what do you think we can do that hadn't already been done?"

"Boys, this is West Texas, cattle country, and all of our lives and throughout our history, back through our ancestors, we have never settled for less than justice. If a coyote is killing your calves, we don't wait for the animal control to trap it and humanely release it back into the wild. If a rattlesnake is eating your chickens, you use your rifle and hang his carcass on the fence. Short and sweet, we take care of our own." Only a nervous shuffling of feet could be heard as dead silence fell over the table. In a still lower voice, barely above a whisper, Bob continued, "As I said earlier, I have a plan, a good one I think. But if anyone here doesn't want to hear it, I suggest you leave now and forget everything you heard here today."

Again, almost dead silence followed his words, only glances and eye contact between the other four huddled together.

After a few moments that everyone seemed to be rationalizing the impact of Bob's presentation, Parker Coburn, usually the least talkative of all, cleared his throat and replied, "You've all been friends of mine for a long time, and to each of you I owe something. Most of all, Bob, I could not have asked for a better friend than you. This is a long stretch for me, for all of us for that matter, but in my heart I know someone has got to do something. This cannot continue in our town. So, I guess what I am saying is, count me in; let's hear the plan."

That statement, unexpected from the usually laid-back oil company owner, simply opened the door for the others to follow. JJ, Pablo, and Mal all followed with affirmative responses. The plan was open for discussion.

Bob Bullock reached into his inside coat pocket, and as he produced five playing cards that he laid on the table, begin to explain the plan, "Gentlemen, I removed five playing cards from a brand-new deck this morning, and purposefully picked these five." He then peeled off the cards one by one and placed them on the table face up: the Ace of Spades, the King of Hearts, the Queen of Diamonds, the Jack of Diamonds and the two of Clubs. The Two of Clubs, known as the Deuce of Clubs in poker hands, is known to be the lowest valued card in a deck of fifty-two.

Bob continued, "My plan is simple. We shuffle and place the cards face down on the table. We then, in random order, each draw a card without revealing it to anyone else. No one." He emphatically repeated, "I mean no one ever divulges what card he drew. Take it home and burn it, cut it into a thousand pieces or whatever; your choice, but destroy it."

"But *Amigo*," Pablo questioned: What happens if we draw what card?"

"Come on, Pablo, don't play dumb with me. You know the deuce is low. Whoever draws the two is responsible for taking care of the problem. No questions asked and no one ever knows who is responsible or how it was done, contracted or whatever. No witnesses, no nothing, just results. Not just Burson, but a lot of surrounding communities are going to be much better off when this little problem has gone away. I suppose you might say, it's one of those rare instances when the ends justify the means."

And once again, an agonizing amount of time passed with each weighing the pros and cons of the plan and, without doubt, the possible life changing experience that could impact their respective lives forever.

This time it was JJ that broke the silence. "Shuffle, Bob, I might as well draw first. As always, I got ranch work to do."

All four had drawn and departed with only minimal expressions of farewell as Bob Bullock lingered. He picked up the last card and without looking at the face of it, returned it to his inner coat pocket. He wasn't sure how long he would wait before finding out which card was his, and the consequence of his plan.

Gail was not at the cashier's counter as he paid his check and left.

Good, he thought, *no nosy questions from Gail this time. That might have been difficult to explain.*

CHAPTER THIRTY-NINE

Sheriff and Police Chief, Third Meeting

Mid-morning, less than three days after their second meeting, Chief Ward Thomason was on the phone with Sheriff Buck Jones again.

"Buck, how 'bout you and I get together for lunch today at Gail's Diner? Think I have something you might like to hear."

"Do some of my best Sherlock Holmes type work while eating; how about 12:30?"

"Good for me, see you there."

At 12:30 p.m. sharp, Ward Thomason and Buck Jones arrived at almost the same instance in the Police Chief's and Sheriff's cars respectively, parking side by side in the west side lot of Gail's Diner.

"Afternoon Ward," as Buck lifted his mighty frame from the Dodge four door sedan.

"Back at you, hungry?"

"Don't I look like I'm always hungry?"

"Well, looking at your fat butt compared to my skinny ass, I'd surmise that Sheriff's pay is a whole lot better than a Police Chief's."

"Guess that's a subject for another day. Let's grab some grub."

Gail, with menus in hand, met the two top law enforcement men as they walked through the door.

"Good Gosh almighty, who in the world is keeping the store? Crime is gonna be running rampant while you two are down here lolly-gagging around."

"Cool it Toots," Buck chided, "comedy and satire, is not your strong suit. However, if the lunch is on the house, I might cancel the raid on this joint I got scheduled for later this evening."

Gail just laughed and asked, "Okay, so much for the humor. Where do you big boys want to sit?"

Ward responded, "How about the one near the back that is sort of out of earshot from the normal crowd?"

"Suits me if it does you chief."

Picking up a couple of place settings as she passed the amply supplied bin, Gail led the two lawmen to the requested back booth.

Once seated, Buck asked, "What you got Ward?"

Lowering his voice and barely audible, Ward replied, "As far as I know, nobody but Phil and I know this. As you probably know, Phil is pretty-close to Gail. A couple of days ago she confided to Phil that about a month ago, she overheard the regular Friday Five talking real low, like us now. They were discussing their mutual dislike for one Little Bob Herring, and someone needed to stop the bleeding in this community caused by him, and the sooner the better. And now the real zinger, she heard Bull tell the others about West

Texas cattle ranching history; about coyotes and rattlesnakes killing calves, chickens, and other small animals. They didn't wait for trappers to take care of the problem; just shot 'em and hung their carcasses on fence lines to rot."

Visibly shaken, Buck was searching for words. "Can't say I was expecting to hear that kind of news. What else did she hear?"

"Well, damnit, this is where the hitch comes in. Seems her little eavesdropping endeavor came to a sudden halt when the cook was calling for help in the kitchen. When she got back to her listening post, they were talking so low she couldn't make out the words. Just told Phil that they all seemed dead serious when they paid the check and left. No good-natured bantering like usual."

Sheriff Jones leaned back in the booth, his rather heavy girth pushing the table a bit closer to Chief Ward, listening closely to the conversation, closed his eyes as he processed the magnitude of all the possibilities that Ward's message had opened. Neither spoke for at least a few minutes.

The silent pondering of the two officers of the law was abruptly interrupted as Gail arrived carrying two large glasses brimming full of ice-tea, both filled with more ice than tea, the norm for Texas tea drinkers.

"What's for lunch, fellows? The beef stew is probably the best thing going today. Cookie's got a real knack for cooking that stew, and the butcher bought up some real good stuff this week. Had a bowl myself a bit ago, and I thought it was delicious, and I'm not easy to please."

Buck smiled at Gail and replied, "Good enough for the owner, gotta be good enough for me."

Ward affirmed, "Good enough for the Sheriff; bound to be good enough for me also."

Gail wheeled around and headed back to the kitchen serving window, clipped the order on the spindle carrying the lunch orders, and moved on to other customers.

Buck leaned forward and lowered his voice until it was barely audible. "Just thinking Ward, wondering if we might be smart just to sit Gail down, lay our cards on the table, and trust her to put a lip on it. Then just plain out ask her and see if she knows any more than what your boy Phil got. 'Course, we could bring her down to your office or mine, but that news would get around faster than a greyhound chasing a rabbit, and that would surely blow down some good behind the scenes detective work we could get done if nobody knew what we're thinking."

"I sure as hell agree with that. The minute she came to yours or my office, the whole dang town would be second guessing every move that we made, and they sure wouldn't spare any time spreading the word."

"How about right after a good bowl of hot steaming stew? Most of the working folks will be getting back on the job and we could just eat slowly, and after a huge slice of that hot apple pie, have a nice social visit with the owner and manager of this fine restaurant."

Gail arrived shortly afterwards with two bowls of beef stew and packaged saltine crackers on a plastic tray held shoulder high with one hand and a pitcher filled with ice and a reasonable amount of sweet tea in the other. "If that's all, I'll check on you two cowboys later." With a mischievous smile and a flirtatious wink, she wheeled around and headed for other duties.

No more shop talk ensued for the next twenty minutes, only two friends enjoying a well-prepared meal.

CHAPTER FORTY

Private Meeting Between the Sheriff, Police Chief, and Gail

Twenty-five minutes later, Gail returned to pick up the dishes and dinnerware. "How was the stew and pie, boys? Good as advertised?"

"Been a while since I had better," Buck said.

"I'll testify to that evaluation," Ward replied. "Good job, Gail. Real nice lunch and thank you very much."

Gail placed the green and white ticket on the table face down and turned to leave when Chief Ward placed his hand on her arm and gently halted her movement. "If you can spare a few minutes now that the noon rush is over, Buck and I would like to discuss something with you in private, please. And in doing so, we would ask you to keep it just between the three of us, as this is extremely important. Most of all, we would sort of pretend we are just socializing about the weather and Burson gossip as usual, if anyone should be inquisitive about our conversation."

"Give me about five minutes and I'll tell Nelda to finish bussing the tables and pass out the checks to the two or three remaining tables. I'll tell her I'm going to be doing some deep steamy gossip with my boy friends. That little story will surely hold water." She departed with more haste than normal.

Less than five minutes later she returned and scooted into the booth next to Ward, who obligingly moved over near the wall side of the seat.

Ward initiated the conversation and summarized everything that he and Buck had discussed, again reiterating the importance of complete confidence required that no one outside of the present parties could know the subject of the discussion. "We are aware of the conversation that you shared recently with Phil regarding your accidental over-hearing the Friday Five a month or so ago. And while I'm thinking about it, please don't be upset with Phil. He would normally take your secret to his grave with him, but we got a murder on our hands and we need all the help we can get. That means no one is out of the question as a suspect. After all, the victim did have more folks in this town with a reason to gun him down than a stray dog has fleas."

Buck, listening intently to his fellow law officer, quietly, but forcefully spoke next. "Gail, as everyone in town knows, every one of the Friday Five, except Bull, has lost a loved one to some act associated with Little Bob. We all know that his parents stuck with him, as almost any parent would do, and had the financial resources required to hire the pricey lawyers that keep him out of the big Brick House at Huntsville and at home and on the street. In this little town of ours just about everybody knows everybody and the biggest percentage of our citizens are just, plain, good old western folks with a deep belief in religion, family and friends." Buck paused for a minute to rethink his next statement.

Meanwhile Gail had sat impassively, showing no emotion one way or the other. Both Buck and Ward were sharing the same thoughts. *Did we make a mistake in confiding this to her? Will she feel obligated to tell Bull or one of the other Five? That would certainly put a monkey-wrench in our plan.* Buck cleared his throat and thought to himself: *What the hell, I've gone this far, so might as well go for broke.*

"Here's the nuts and bolts of this problem Gail. We know each one of these gentlemen personally, and no one wants to believe that anyone of those five would pull the trigger." A long pause before he continued. "But the fact is, someone here in Burson either did the deed themselves or, more than likely, paid a professional to do the dirty work for them. Either way, Ward and I have a job to do. We took an oath to uphold the law, and so help me Lord, that's what I intend to do. And I know Ward feels the same way. We neither one will get any pleasure in putting pressure on you, but the murder was committed, and we have to do our dead level best to find and bring the killer to justice."

Both men sat motionless, searching Gail's eyes for some sense as to what she must be thinking. Moments passed with no one moving or making a sound.

Gail broke the somber atmosphere of the moment. Picking up her now cooled down coffee mug, she downed a couple of ounces, squared up in her seat and spoke without hesitance: "Boys, I love those guys like brothers. They have been coming in here for years and I met most of them when they moved here, exception being Parker and Mal. But having said that, as much as I disliked the little son-a-bitch, God rest his soul. I do not condone murder as the way to solve a problem. It goes against my religion and general concept of right from wrong. Therefore, if it were my own brother, I would still do whatever I could to help bring justice in this case." She paused for another sip of coffee. "I'll be glad to answer any questions you have and try to provide more information if I can; and believe it or not, I can keep my mouth shut when I have to, and I would say that this is one of those times."

Buck, heaving a sigh of relief, was the first to respond: "I'm really glad to hear you say that Gail. And I know I'm speaking for Ward also, that you will never be involved except in the strictest confidence."

Ward reached over and gently laid his hand on hers: "That is an absolute positive. We are just looking for a way to get some leads without involving you publicly. We all have been friends for a long, long time and I, for one, intend to keep it that way for many, many more years. Now, with that out of the way, can you tell us just what you heard from the Friday Five gathering?"

Gail was used to using a lot of slang and good-natured banter with numerous West Texas colloquialism among her mostly blue-collar customers but, as a matter of fact, she was an avid reader and had a great command of the English language that most people never heard.

Speaking slowly, she laid out the information that she had previously confided to her friend, Officer Phil. It matched the story almost exactly to what Phil had reported to Ward. She further explained why her curiosity compelled her to listen in on the conversation. It was the fact that they never come in on Tuesday, hence the name Friday Five, and the somber attitude that was so evident from the time they arrived. Further reliving the Friday Five meeting, she stated, "Bull, as usual, was in complete command of the meeting. But usually, he is as loud as the proverbial bullhorn, but this time he was speaking in measured sentences in a low, almost whispering voice. The part of the conversation, and I'm positive that I heard this just as he said it and was emphatic that he meant it, was the part that when the justice system fails us, and sometimes, we West Texans just have got to take care of the matter ourselves. And I think that this might be one of those times."

"Anything else come to mind?" Ward asked.

"No, not really, and as I told Phil, I sort of got called away by Cookie just when it was getting really interesting. It was really quiet when they paid their check and all quickly left the diner, just unusually polite with no back-and-forth banter. They were real, real strange acting that day. That is one of the main reasons I kind of thought I had to share it with somebody, and Phil was the first one that I thought of."

Gail set motionless for a few moments without speaking.

Ward offered a matter-of fact statement. "I would hate to think it could be one of those five. They all are outstanding citizens of Burson, but you really never know what lengths some folks will go to right a wrong, particularly, when it involves the loss of a friend or family member."

Pausing, she patiently waited for one of the two law officers to continue with their questions.

Chief Ward turning his attention to Sheriff Buck and without speaking, just a shrug of the shoulders indicating neither one of the two officers had any other questions to ask of Gail.

Returning his attention to Gail, "No further questions Gail, but both Buck and I can only express our sincere gratitude. You are a valuable member of our community."

Sheriff Buck slipped out of his side of the booth and almost immediately, Gail arose from her seat as well. Police Chief Ward Thomason slid over to the aisle side of the booth and, in stark contrast to the heavier Sheriff Jones, nimbly jumped to his feet.

Ward extended a warm handshake to Gail. "Gail Honey, I thank you so much for your cooperation. We will keep you in the loop. By the way, you forgot to bring us a check."

Neither of the two officers had been aware of Gail picking up the ticket and putting it into her pocket a few minutes earlier.

Gail stood motionless for a few moments without speaking. "This is on the house boys, had a pretty good week, and besides, I'll just add on a little extra next time."

Buck responded with a great big hug. "Much thanks Gail, and you might have just provided the tip that brings this mess to an early conclusion. Take care, now, and we will talk again soon." A goodbye wave with his big Stetson and he, along with Ward, left the diner.

As the two walked to their respective autos, Buck seemed deep in thought before suggesting, "Ward, suppose you and I mosey on over to my office for just a little more brainstorming before we call it a day with each other."

"Probably a good idea to formulate some new strategy in light of what Gail confided to us. I'll drive around a few minutes and get on the two-way and sort of check in with my desk clerk and just make sure no irons are burning in some fire that I need to know about. That way, if anyone was noticing us back at Gail's and was wondering what was going on, might throw them off a bit."

"Do what you got to do and see you when you get there, no rush required." Buck then squeezed his near two hundred-fifty-pound body into his Chevrolet Sheriff's car and departed.

CHAPTER FORTY-ONE

A Secret Meeting Between the Sheriff and Police Chief

The big clock on the corner outside the West Texas First National Bank had just struck 4:30 p.m. when Ward pulled into the rear parking lot behind the Sheriff's office. He quickly departed his auto and entered the rear door of the Sheriff's office and entered Buck's private office, bypassing the receptionist's outer office.

"Pull up a chair Ward, and let's see if we can make some sense out of this situation."

Ward grabbed the nearest one, a rather well-worn black leather covered chair and leaned back to listen.

"Seems to me," Buck began, "as I said over at Gail's, four of those guys had a dang good reason to see Little Bob done in. Since you seemed to go along with that line of reasoning, who would you think, assuming for the moment that is one of those four, would be the most likely to pull the trigger, or hire some to do it?"

"Been thinking about that ever since we left there. It's a tough call, and as you say assuming that it is one of the four.

However, I been thinking that if it came out of that group, I would not completely rule out Bull. After all, according to Gail, Bull was the one that suggested that justice should be served by our own. I'll admit, he doesn't have the motive of the other four, but Bull strikes me as one who will back up what he says."

"Sure, can't argue that point!" Buck shook his head in approval, "Sure can't."

Ward continued, "Back to your original question, before I muddied the waters, I suppose if I had to pick one; I guess that I would say Mal. You know, he really took it hard when, as everyone knows, Little Bob paid-off that young Patterson girl to take that rap for him in that drunk-driving accident that killed Mal's mom Carolyn. Besides that, he's got the balls to do it."

"Yeh, and I wouldn't rule out Palo," Buck said. "He and Rita really had it in for him after that little failed abortion episode. However, I guess now that I think about it a little more, I would say that because of their strong religious belief and history, he probably couldn't do it."

There was a short pause before Buck added, "What about Parker? He seems way too nice and I've never seen him lose his temper. Course, he did catch Little Bob swindling him out of a pretty good hunk of cash, back when they were partners in some sort of oil transferring business. I guess that was another one that Little Bob, with big city lawyers and a fat payoff, was able to wiggle himself out of."

"Right," Ward echoed, "But don't forget the tension between the two over Betty Jean. And you know Parker had to take it real hard when he got wind of those drunken rages Little Bob had over the years with Betty Jean, taking some real spousal abuse, but would never testify against him."

"Yep, no doubt about it, Parker took it real hard when Betty Jean left him and married Little Bob. It was so obvious that Parker really loved her, and as far as that is concerned, still does."

"Copy that, Sheriff. So now what's next?"

"Well," he paused for a moment gathering his thoughts, "I suppose the next step is for your guys and my guys start finding out where all the parties were on the night in question. Then when we got all the facts to the best of our knowledge, we consider calling them in and see if their story matches ours."

Ward rose from his chair. "It's been a stressful day, and I'm calling it a day. The missus should have dinner on the stove by now, so I just want to clear my head and save it for another time." He picked up his hat from Buck's desk and departed. "Later," was Ward's departing remark.

"Enjoy and tell the real chief hello for me." Buck leaned back in his swivel chair and reflected on the day's events. Even the thought that anyone of the Friday Five, personal friends and outstanding citizens could be implicated in something as brutal as murder, was weighing heavily on his mind. This was not going to be easy by any means.

Chapter Forty-Two

Deputy Randy Checks Out a Possible Suspect

Almost a month had passed with only minimal exchange of information between Chief Ward and Sheriff Buck. On a Monday morning late in August, the abrupt ringing of the personal phone in Chief Ward's office interrupted the Chief and Officer Phil's usual Monday meeting over coffee; as the two exchanged small talk of the previous weekend's events.

The incoming call was from the personal office phone of Sheriff Jones. "Ward, Buck here."

Cradling the phone with his shoulder as he was soon stirring his steaming coffee, attempting to cool it enough for sipping, he responded, "And a cheery good morning to you also, Buck. What's up?"

Without acknowledging the chief's obvious intent of humor, "I suppose that Phil is there with you?"

"That's correct. How can we help you?"

"Randy is here with me, and we've got some things I want to put to rest. Mr. Bob Herring Sr. was my first call this

morning, and he's getting pretty danged restless about the progress of our investigation. I can understand his concern. Even though he knew Little Bob was far from being an angel, he was their only son; and he wants to see justice done sooner than later. And on top of that, even though he's been out the business for quite a while, he still has some clout in Austin and is considering hiring a high-dollar private investigator. And we need that like we need the proverbial hole in the head."

"I'll second that in capital letters, so, where you headed with this?" Ward asked.

"Hold that question for just a second, Ward." He turned to face his deputy: "Randy, can you hike it over to Abilene this morning and check out that lead and get back by three or four?"

Deputy Randy Spears shaking his head affirmatively, "I can leave now and should get what we need and still have a couple of hours left when I get back."

"Good Randy, haul ass, but don't get a speeding ticket." He was laughing softly as he returned his attention to the Police Chief: "I think when Randy confirms one more lead we've been chasing, we can narrow this field down quite a bit. Can you bring Phil and anything you got since our last meeting, and let's pin down a few things?"

"Phil and I will keep our slate open. Just call when Randy gets back."

"Great, will do." Sheriff Buck Jones, pleased with what he hoped would be a turning point in the investigation of one Little Bob Herring's murder, pushed back in his chair and closed his eyes to spend a few minutes relaxing before resuming the normal business of the day.

Deputy Randy's lead had just come about a couple of days earlier. Entering the local convenience store he was greeted by longtime clerk Marshall Johnson. "How's it going today Randy? Anything new on the Herring investigation?"

"Well not anything I could talk about, but we're still looking for leads hoping something fruitful will turn up."

Sacking the snacks Randy had just purchased, Marshall added to the dialogue, "I've sort of been meaning to tell you something that happened shortly before the murder that might be useful."

"I'm all ears, what you got?"

"It was sort of a slow day, so I decided it was a good time we go out and clean the tops off the gas pumps. This guy drove up to the other pump and started filling up his pickup. I noticed and mentioned to him what a nice pickup he was driving. He thanked me and then replied that he was pleased with his decision to buy that brand and model. He then reached into his pocket and pulled out a handful of large domination bills and paid me in cash while we were still outside. The amount he owed what's $29 even and he gave me $30 it told me to keep the change."

Pausing to turn on a pump for a customer, he continued his recollection of the conversation by attempting to quote his questions. "By the way, just wondering if you might know of some ranch land that might be available for deer hunting. I just drove in from Abilene after someone told me that this area had several hundred acres of good hunting ground. Particularly, they mentioned the Herring Ranch. Could you give me directions and possibly someone to contact to see if it would be available?"

Listening and now really paying attention, he said "Sounds like this is something we ought to look into. Sure wish we had a little more information about this guy."

Completing his transaction with Randy, he offered this one more observation regarding this person's pickup. He did not notice the size or brand of the tires on the pickup but did get something that might be of interest. His license plate number ended in 3115. The reason it was significant to him was because it was the same as his house number.

After the drive to Abilene, and arriving to the courthouse, he entered the license bureau section. Explaining his reason for being there, the clerk researched and quickly found the name of the person who bought the license and his address.

After driving a few miles to a nearby rural community and to the address that he had been given, he was able to interview the person of interest. During the extensive interview it was obvious to Randy that the person he was interviewing was open and cooperative. He loved hunting and had just recently lost his deer lease that he had used for many previous years, and the trip to Burson was just what he said it was, to locate a new lease.

Satisfied that the interview confirmed that the person of interest was not in any way involved in the murder case that he was investigating, he thanked the gentleman for his cooperation and said goodbye.

He was disappointed in one sense because another lead went nowhere, but in another sense, he was pleased to find out this gentleman was not involved. Randy began his return drive to Burson.

CHAPTER FORTY-THREE

Officer Phil Discovers A Possible Lead

August in Texas is no picnic for the weak of heart. Ninety plus degrees, even often exceeding one hundred degrees, was more a norm than an exception. So, it was just a few days after Buck and Chief Ward's last meeting that Officer Phil Hawkins parked his black-and-white police cruiser in the local Safeway parking lot and entered the store to purchase a bag of ice and a carton of soft drinks to replenish the small snack room in the police office.

After filling his grocery bag, also containing a few packages of cookies and other snacks that he did not have the willpower to refuse, he was returning to his cruiser as two locally known Hispanic workers were just exiting their parked pickup.

"Hey Mannie and Francisco, hot enough for you two cowboys, or does it need to warm up about another ten degrees for you guys to get comfortable?" he questioned kiddingly.

"*Sí, Amigo*. You know us wetbacks, the hotter the better," they responded as both laughed.

After the mutually light-hearted exchange, Phil continued to his parked cruiser and loaded the sack of refreshments into the rear seat. As he opened the front door to enter the driver's side, he suddenly stopped as something popped into his mind like the proverbial "lightbulb." He stood silently for about a minute, gathering his thoughts, and talking to himself, "Did I just see something or am I just imagining I saw something?" He paused for perhaps another minute processing his thoughts before shutting the car door and walking back to the pickup, the two Hispanics had just parked. A Chevrolet three-quarter-ton pickup, probably a 1966 or 1967, dark blue in color, and with four matching Firestone 310-225 rain thread tires, with still deep threads, was taunting his suspicions right before his eyes.

Like a puzzle beginning to form before his eyes, he suddenly remembered a story circulating a few weeks earlier about an intense argument between Little Bob Herring and some Hispanic workers he had contracted to repair fences surrounding some of the oil tanks and pits on his property. Another piece of the unsolved puzzle popped into his mind as he noticed a large pair of rubber boots stuffed upside down between the cab and the bed, as was common for laborers to keep a pair handy in case of having to work in muddy conditions.

Now realizing he might be onto something significant, he decided to proceed a little further with his now possible new lead into the Herring murder. Pretending to have forgotten some items he had wanted to purchase, he returned to the Safeway store to "accidentally" bump into Mannie and Francisco again. He located them on the can goods aisle stacking up a cart full of their weekly food supply.

"Forgot the peanut butter and crackers," he explained as he greeted the two again.

"*Sí,* me forgetful also, that why I carry list," replied Mannie.

Phil responded with a bit of small talk while studying Mannie's stature and weight. "Approximately five-nine and one-fifty to one-sixty tops." He observed as he continued the conversation. "As he studied his feet, he estimated size nine, possibly a bit more, but surely not a size twelve or thirteen as he had suspected the shooter might be. However, larger boots might have initially belonged to someone else and could just be the handy item for a disguise that the killer needed."

Having completed his excuse for shopping, and not knowing what else to do at this time, he returned to his car and headed back to the station. Driving, he still could not decide if he should share his suspicions, or just go it alone for a while.

CHAPTER FORTY-FOUR

Officer Phil Discusses his Concerns of a Possible Suspect

The following morning, after a sleepless night wondering if maybe he had stumbled onto a solid lead in the murder investigation with the two Hispanics, he was undecided as to what course of action he should take from this point forward. Should he discuss it with the chief, with nothing more than just a nagging suspicion, or should he just conduct his own private investigation, unofficial, until he had something more solid to discuss. That line of reasoning quickly became a no-brainer when he realized what Chief Ward would say if he had knowingly concealed any lead, much less than the most publicized murder investigation in the whole county, and even perhaps the state.

After gulping down the last drop of his second cup of coffee, he rose from his desk and knocked outside of the open door of his chief's office.

"Got a minute Chief Ward?" he asked.

"Sure Phil, and when we are not in public, and it's just you and me, you know it's always just plain old Ward."

"Yes sir, Ward, and I appreciate that. However, I don't want to get out of the habit of being respectful of your position. Having said that, I need to share something that happened yesterday, and get your take on it."

"Lay it on me, son, I'm all ears."

Phil spent the next several minutes recounting his chance encounter with the two Hispanic workers, and the resemblance to the pickup and tires that had been linked to the possible suspect in the Herring murder. He also mentioned the possible rumor about the run in between the two and Little Bob Herring during some fence construction. He also conveyed his suspicion regarding the oversized rubber boots. That might be the possible explanation regarding the unlikely disparity between the suspects size and weight and the unusually large foot size.

"Not sure how to tell this, Phil, but this requires the utmost discretion. JJ Stevens came to me a couple of months ago and related the story to me. However, according to JJ, it's much more involved than the rumor you just reported. Everyone knows that Mannie and Francisco work for JJ and they are both illegal and have been here for many years. Both have families and are honest as the day is long, excellent workers and extremely dependable. JJ pays them a salary and furnishes them one of the old houses on the ranch. He additionally pays the electric, provides them with butane for heating, and necessary appliances. Long story short, their salary is modest, but he does look after their needs."

Following a brief interruption from his secretary, Chief Ward continued, "Over the years, in slack times, meaning not having baby calves or cattle shipping times, he has let neighbors use their services and pick up some cheap labor, which helps both the neighbors and Mannie and Francisco.

Seems that was the case when Little Bob asked JJ if he could use the two for a few days to help with some fencing around some of his oil leases. Of course, as you may or may not know, all of those producing oil wells produce some drip gas. All you got to do is drain the water from the separator and have a five-gallon gas can handy and pick you up some free fuel for your truck. Not good on your engine so most pumpers just dump it back into the well and forget it, as it does not add up to much in the overall production. However, again according to JJ, Little Bob accused the two, Mannie and Francisco, of stealing the drip from him. Well, anyway, that did not sit well with the two. Mannie, particularly, was really offended that his honesty was being questioned, and proceeded by demanding an apology. Apparently, things got a little heated from there and ended up with Little Bob getting a revolver out of his truck and threatened to shoot Mannie. Mannie wisely retreated, picked up his tools and drove away. Little Bob shot at the pickup as they drove away. Don't know if he was trying to hit them or not, but it did leave a dent in the tailgate of the truck."

Chief Ward rose from his desk, walked to a small table in the corner of his office, and poured himself a glass of water from the ice filled pitcher.

"Glass of water, Phil?" Ward asked.

"No thanks, Ward, I had two cups of java just before I came into your office."

"Well, to continue my story, or rather JJ's story, Mannie came straight to JJ and recounted the full story to him. Well, not having any love lost between Little Bob and JJ anyway, he immediately high-tailed it over to Little Bob's place and proceeded to read him the riot act. Obviously upset about what he deemed to be a way too far out accusation of his employee's honesty and integrity, he let Little Bob know in no uncertain terms he knew how to use a revolver, a shotgun, and a rifle to boot. And that he was a damned better shot than him and he was not afraid to use either one of the three if pushed."

Ward leaned forward in his chair. "What I'm saying, Phil, is that makes one more suspect that we have to consider. But I'm damn sure hoping and praying that this turns out to be a false lead."

Chapter Forty-Five

Phillip and Malcolm Morris

Phillip was the sole owner or Rancher's Best Friend Feed Store and had been so since the death of his older brother, Paul. The two brothers had started the business some sixteen years ago and was the only feed store in the area, therefore becoming quite "well heeled" as was the local custom to describe one's financial status. Paul's untimely passing was due to lung cancer, the beast of all illnesses. A long-time widower, Paul had no children, so the entire estate was left to his only living relative, Phillip.

Phillip and Malcolm Morris, best known as Mal Morris, and only someone new in the area would ever use the word Malcolm in his presence. Mal, at forty-three years of age, was one humungous human being, tipping the scales at two-seventy-five and at six-foot-four towered over most around him. Having grown up on one of the smaller ranches just south of Burson, Mal had graduated from Burson High and after an outstanding career as an offensive and defensive lineman, was offered and accepted a scholarship to play football for the Hardin Simmons Cowboys in nearby Abilene, Texas.

After a stellar career with the Cowboys, Mal proudly earned his degree in ranch management. Intent on returning to his roots as a rancher, Mal's longtime ambition and intentions got sidelined when his older brother talked him into joining him in opening a new enterprise.

The new enterprise, all Paul's idea, was to purchase a flatbed truck with attachable rails that would be ideal for hauling feed to the many local ranches in this and adjoining counties, was that he and Mal would jointly secure a loan from the local bank to purchase a new truck.

Although most of the larger ranches raised their own feed, coastal bermuda as first choice, there were more than enough smaller operations that did not have enough acreage in cultivation to produce their own and had to rely on outside sources to feed their cattle. This was particularly true during moisture starved West Texas summers. Paul and Mal could purchase feed from the larger ranchers nearby, and in years that it was not available, shift their resources to different parts of the state, or even nearby New Mexico, and haul it directly to their local customers. During their growing years, adding food and medicine for local pet owners could prove to be a profitable addition to their business.

A meeting in the First National Bank with the president and chief loan officer, Bob Bullock, where their presentation to obtain a loan to open a new business in Burson, was quickly approved. Bob also promised additional financial help for future growth. He rose from his chair, shook their hands, and wished them great success.

Thus, begins the story of a long-time friendship between the then young, newest loan officer at the Burson First National Bank, Bob Bullock, and Mal Morris.

Chapter Forty-Six

Phillip, Mal, and Little Bob Herring Jr.

Phillip and Mal Morris had more than a common interest in the fate of the young Little Bob Herring. Ten years earlier Phillip and Paul experienced the nightmare of having their mother killed in a car crash while returning from church one evening. Little Bob Herring and his date for the evening was traveling along County Road 923 after a night of partying in the nearby town of Abilene. Little Bob, as usual, had experienced a night of excessive drinking and was speeding as he approached a narrow bridge on the highway. Carolyn Morris was approaching the same bridge at the same time. Little Bob, under the influence, and with minimal reflexes, misjudged the approaching car and swerved into the center lane of the narrow bridge. Blinded by the oncoming headlights of the approaching car, Little Bob frantically turned the steering wheel to the right attempting to avoid a collision, but he was too late in doing so.

Carolyn Morris was killed instantly upon impact. Little Bob Herring and his young companion Janie Preston were both injured and unable to exit the vehicle as both the driver's and passenger doors were jammed. Janie was bleeding from

severe scratches and bruises on her forehead and shoulder. Little Bob was bruised and bleeding as well but was more concerned about Janie's condition. After a few moments of comforting each other, Little Bob was able to crawl into the back seat and exit the smashed vehicle. Still groggy from the impact of the crash and the after effect of too much booze, he had Janie hand him a flashlight from the dash pocket and walked over to examine the other demolished car and check on the condition of the occupants. Carolyn Morris, driver, and sole occupant was lifeless and nearly decapitated by the steering wheel that was lodged in her neck. Sickened at the site he was he witnessing, he turned away and began to vomit violently.

Somewhere between attempting to contain his sickness, clear his head and decide what to do next, he returned to the car where Janie was still unable to open her passenger side door. Crawling into the back seat again, he reached over and retrieved the keys and then opened the trunk to retrieve a toolbar, which he then used to pry open the jammed door and assist Janie to her feet.

Standing in the darkness, and after both had decided that their injuries were not life threatening, both discussed what to do next. The only option that seemed to be logical was to just wait until someone came along to assist them.

With Little Bob's thinking becoming more rational by the moment, it dawned on him that this would surely cost him his license to drive. This obviously would be considered by the law force to be his fault and his previous DUI would be the final "straw that broke the camel's back." He had to do something and do it quickly.

The proverbial "light in his head" came on and a plan was quickly devised. He would ask Janie to accept the blame by claiming to be driving because he realized he should not drink and drive.

Selling that plan to Janie proved to be a little more difficult than he had expected. At first refusing to go along with that plan, she finally gave in and consented to do so, but only after Little Bob had sweetened the pot. Being the daughter of a modest income family, and never having a car of her own to drive, the offer of a brand-new car with complete ownership was just too good to pass up.

So, one more time in his young life, Little Bob "dodged a bullet."

County Road 923 normally did not have much traffic, but a car traveling toward Burson caught the attention of Little Bob and he frantically waved the flashlight bringing the car to a stop. A young man, Jon Baker, like Little Bob, was returning home from a date with his Abilene girlfriend. He quickly exited his car and offered his help.

A decision, at Little Bob's urging, was for Jon to transport Janie to the Burson Hospital. After notifying her parents, he would notify the police as well as the Sheriff's office, and they would come to the wreckage. Little Bob would stay behind and, with the flashlight, warn any approaching traffic.

Not knowing the identity of the driver of the smashed car he could only grieve, and still one more time, face up to the fact that he was responsible for an innocent person's death. A lot of people are going to really be unhappy with this accident and the driver that caused it. And two of those with the most to lose, and who would not forget nor forgive, Phillip and Mal Morris.

A long sad night was still in store for a lot of Burson residents.

Chapter Forty-Seven

Parker Suspects Fraudulent Dealings with Bob Herring Jr.

Parker and Little Bob had been business acquaintances for several years now, and often used Parker's office to discuss contracts, progress, and setbacks. Herring's company had almost been the exclusive contractor for clean-out, rod, pipe and pump repair for Parker's numerous oil and gas producing wells. Parker's company owned no pulling unit equipped trucks, relying solely on contractor services as needed for those services. Over the years the two men had jointly negotiated transactions for acquiring leases and now owned equal shares in a half-dozen producing wells.

Based on just the traditional Texas handshake, Parker's office was responsible for inventory, the monthly reports to the Texas Oil and Gas Commission, the distribution of working interest and royalty checks, and other everyday legal work required of an oil and gas producer. Herring's responsibility was, through his employees, the two or three times a week maintenance at the well site, gauging the storage tanks, logging the results, and the trucking transfer of oil from the tanks to the refinery as needed.

What had begun as a comfortable relationship between the two limited partners, based on a mutual respect, began to take on a different tone in the later years of their partnership. Both business and social contact between the two became more infrequent, and there was a sense of distrust developing in Parker's mind about his partner. Recent fluctuations in the normal twice-a-week storage tanks reports were becoming a cause for concern. Producing wells that had been reliably stable for months, even years, were suddenly showing significantly lower production of oil.

Thoughts of suspicion and puzzlement were randomly flowing through Parker's mind. *"Something fishy's going on here . . . can't quite figure this out, but something just doesn't seem right. I just wonder what the hell's going on?"*

His silent thoughts evolved into talking aloud, in barely a whisper, and to no one in particular: *Whatever it is, I gotta get to the bottom of this; and pretty dang quick!*

For the following two months, Parker continued to monitor the reports from the three or four oil wells that he suspected Little Bob was fraudulently reporting. His mind kept searching the numerous scenarios that how the illegal transaction could be taking place. After much anguish, he decided on a plan of action.

Sandy Smith, a trusted long time contract field employee, if someone should ask, was taking a two-week vacation. Being single and living alone, he could easily assume the role of private detective. Only he and Parker would share this secret. His job was to discreetly follow one or two of the tanker trucks owned by Little Bob and keep notes of time and locations of pick-up and delivery. Also, three of the tanks owned by Parker, the suspected ones of falsely reported cheating, would be gauged daily. After the two weeks of monitoring an accurate total the oil produced it could be used for later comparison to Little Bob's report.

Two weeks after his first job being a private eye, Sandy reported to Parker the results of his investigation. It was as expected, Parker was being swindled by little Bob Herring. In real terms, little Bob was stealing oil from tanks belonging to Parker and selling it as if it were from his own tanks, and apparently had been doing so for several months.

Parker again asked Sandy for complete secrecy regarding his role as a private detective, thanked him for a job well done, and then rewarded him with extra money for his service.

CHAPTER FORTY-EIGHT

Parker Accuses Little Bob of Stealing

Little Bob Herring was standing in front of a file cabinet searching through some papers in his office, located on the north side of the large Herring Ranch house, when he was interrupted by the ringing of his private phone sitting on his desk. He quickly walked back to his phone, picked up the receiver and answered. "Little Bob here, what can I do for you?"

"Bob, this is Parker. Any chance you could drop by my office sometime today for a little meeting? Got some things to discuss with you."

"Sure thing, Parker, need to pick up things at the store this afternoon anyway. So is 2:30 or 3:00 p.m. okay with you?"

"Fine with me. I'll tell Mary Francis to send you on in."

"I'll be there. see you."

True to his word, at 2:45 p.m. Little Bob greeted Mary Frances with a bit of small talk before she politely informed him that Mr. Coburn was expecting him. "Please go on in."

After a brief exchange of greetings, Parker asked Little Bob to review the papers laying on his desk that he had carefully arranged in order by dates. The papers were those oil tank gauging reports given to Parker by Little Bob compared to the ones that Parker's detective had obtained.

Little Bob's denial of any wrongdoing quickly turned to anger as the two men engaged in a heated discussion over the authenticity of the reports. As the words of the argument became louder and louder, the office staff was fully aware that something was happening between the two, and it certainly was not good.

At one point little Bob was overheard to say Parker was only jealous of him by marrying his one time secretary Betty Jean. Parker had responded by saying the only reason he would not send him to prison was because it would be too hard on Betty Jean and the girls.

His face red from anger and with his fists clinched, he had responded to Parker by saying that death was better than going to prison.

Parker was also enraged, "Careful what you ask for, I just might make that happen."

No further words were spoken as little Bob abruptly turned and left the office.

Parker, looking out of his office window, unsure of what his next move should be.

CHAPTER FORTY-NINE

The Split Aces Ranch

JJ, formal name John Joseph Stephens, always wore a big Stetson hat that partially shielded a tan wrinkled leather like face that was the trademark of the life of a hardworking cowboy. Ranch life was the only life JJ had ever known. JJ, head honcho of the Split Aces Ranch, was the third generation Stevens to be owner and manager of the sprawling twenty-two section working cattle ranch. Story goes that JJ's grandfather had a small spread and as was often the case in those earlier pioneering years, many acres of land changed from one owner to another on the turn of a card. The elder Stevens just eked out a "keep your head above water" living by raising less than a hundred purebred white face herefords each year. Always loving card games, usually once a week in the background of Presley's Barber Shop, Billy Joe Stevens had honed his card play skills as tight as a finetuned fiddle. So, in the twilight years of his life, and after selling sixty-five yearlings at the local cattle auction, Billy Joe Senior pocketed twenty-five one-hundred-dollar bills and headed for Reno, Nevada, and his first ever big time gambling experience.

After an uneventful three days of trying his luck at one casino after another, poker, regular stud, and seven-card, he never got ahead or behind significantly enough to brag or complain. Either way. It was just a bit of a ho-hum, three-day gambling spree with novices and professionals both in the mix. But day four, now that's a different story. Billy Joe hit Benny Binion's Casino around three in the afternoon, parked his behind on a blackjack stool in the third base position and finally got the gambler's dream, a winning streak as big as the Texas prairie sky over his beloved ranch back near Burson. At twelve o'clock midnight, right on the button, BJ as he was often called, pushed in all the chips he had won during that once-in-a-lifetime winning streak and went for the showdown. He had drawn split aces and the dealer was showing a five of hearts as the up-card. The tension rose and he could feel the tingling in his spine, the sort of feeling you get when you look over the edge of a tall building, as he had risked it all with a double down. BJ drew the face cards on his first ace for a sure win or tie, and the four on his second ace. The correct play would be to stay, as the dealer was showing the five. No backing down now, BJ signaled the dealer for a second hit. The six of spades was the card that pushed the testing right out of his spine. The dealer turned up at seven, drew a face card for the second hit, and BJ simply let out a deep breath and reach for his drink.

Turning $2,500 into near $60,000 within four days was turning rags into riches for the elderly hardworking cowboy from Texas. Only a few months later, and after a bit of shrewd real estate purchases, BJ's little four sections of a working ranch became the rambling twenty-two section ranch widely known as the Split Aces.

JJ's father, Billy Joe Stephens Jr., had inherited the Split Aces Ranch from his father who had passed away early in life. Like his father Billy Joe Jr. also fathered only one child, John Joseph Stephens. BJ, Jr., who had enlisted in the Marine Corps during the Korean War in the early 50s, tragically lost his life while fighting in action for his country.

Still a young man and devastated about the loss of his father, JJ was fully capable of taking over the reins of the Split Aces Ranch. He dedicated his life to managing the vast estate that he had inherited and caring for his mother who was not in good health. Only a few years later, cancer took its toll and his mother passed away at an early age, leaving him as the only remaining member of the Stevens family.

CHAPTER FIFTY

Three Young Boys Caught Fishing on the Herring Lake

On an early Saturday morning in late spring of the year, three young Hispanic boys, ages 14 through 16, with fishing poles and backpacks, were returning to their homes on the Split Aces Ranch after an all-night sleepout and early morning fishing trip. The Lake that the young boys were fishing in was known to be a private lake that Little Bob kept well stocked with small mouth bass for his friends and business associates.

Still walking on Herring Ranch property, the three boys were so happy talking about their night outing and the success that they had in catching several small mouth bass. A special dinner of fried fish for their evening meal was already making their mouths water.

Back at the Herring Ranch House Little Bob was having his morning coffee on the east porch when two of his ranch hands rode up.

Arising from his chair, "What's happening boys, need a real cup of java?"

"Nah, nothing real bad Boss, but thought you would like to know. Seems like you got some uninvited guests fishing in your private lake, three young'uns, Hispanics, from the Split Aces I'm pretty sure."

"Hey Roy, you and Jimbo saddle up Smokey while I get my jeans and boots on and we will just visit these young fishermen and put the fear of God in 'em."

Only a few minutes later the three horsemen led by Little Bob on his favorite horse Smokey, were in a slow gallop towards the location the three young boys were last seen. Having seen the approaching horsemen, the boys began to run toward the fence separating the two ranches. Youthful legs enabled the boys to run extremely fast, but it was no match for the galloping horses that quickly surrounded them.

Little Bob, speaking to what he thought to be the oldest of the three boys, "What are you young brats doing on my property, just having a little hiking trip or have you been fishing in my Lake that everyone knows is a private lake?"

"Yes, sir, we just knew that it was a good lake for fishing, but we didn't know it was private lake. We just wanted to catch some fish for dinner tonight. I hope you understand, sir, we didn't mean no harm to anybody."

"Don't start lying to me you little piece of crap, or I'll get off of this horse and spank your bottom so hard that you'll not want to sit down and eat fish or anything else for dinner."

The older of the three boys, Luis, had just about had all the threats he could stand from the Herring Ranch owner and turned to the two younger friends and in a voice loud enough that he could clearly be heard. "Forget about him and let's go home."

The other two young boys paused briefly and then began to follow their leader, intent on returning to their home as quickly as possible.

"And just where do you think you're going you little fart?" Luis, a standout athlete in both football and track at Burson High, was not backing down from the now out-of-control Little Bob Herring.

"We're going back home, and we're not coming back. Everyone knows that you're just a bully, you cheat, and you're cruel to other people." Luis led the way and the other two followed without saying anything to anyone.

Little Bob, getting angrier by the moment, reined his horse, Smokey, in front of the boys as they attempted to walk home. Using his fishing pole, Luis spanked the rear end of the horse in front of him causing him to lurch sideways almost unseating Little Bob. By now completely losing his temper, Little Bob righted his seat in the saddle, jerked the reins around his horse's neck, and charged into the three young boys. All three were knocked to the ground, but only Luis suffered a severe injury. Smokey, being constantly spurred by his rider, not only pushed the boys down but also stepped on Luis's leg. The bold snap of the bone, loud enough to be clearly heard by the ranch hands, was evidence of a compound fracture.

Roy and Jimbo, for the most part, having stayed in the background during their boss's raging interaction with the young boys, now moved in to help control the violence that was rapidly getting out of hand. Roy positioned his horse between Smokey and the little boys still laying on the ground. Jimbo was attempting to treat Luis and refrain him from moving his fractured leg.

Regaining some composure, Little Bob, leaving Roy and Jimbo to tend to and comfort the injured young boys, would ride back to the Ranch House, and arrange for an ambulance. Less than thirty minutes later an ambulance, summoned by Little Bob, made its way across the ranch property to the injured parties. After injecting a pain reliever, a splint was applied to his fractured leg and Luis was carefully loaded into the ambulance and began the journey to the Burson Emergency Room.

Mannie and Francisco, respective fathers of the boys would be notified by the Emergency Room staff. JJ Stephens would also be advised regarding what had happened on the Herring Ranch and how Little Bob was involved.

Chapter Fifty-One

JJ Stephens Phones Little Bob

Unable to communicate with the families of the young boys with only scratches and bruises and the more seriously injured in the incident, Luis Garcia, a staff member at the Burson Emergency Room contacted JJ and requested his help to notify the parents of the young boys. Both parents, the Garcias and the Gonzaleses were in a short driving distance from JJ's home and shortly after being informed were on their way to the hospital. The two younger boys were treated for minor injuries and released immediately to their respective families.

Satisfied that young Luis Garcia was in the good hands of the doctors tending to his injuries, JJ made a quick trip to Sheriff Buck Jones's office. Arriving at the office he informed the secretary of the importance of his visit and requested an immediate meeting with the Sheriff. He did not have to wait as Buck opened his office door and noticing JJ standing at the reception desk, extended his hand for a handshake and greeted him: "Hey JJ, what brings you into town? Shouldn't you be out playing cowboy about this time of day?"

"Hi Buck, got some serious stuff to talk about. Can you spare a few minutes in private?"

"No problem. Come on into my office JJ." Turning to his secretary as he continued to his office: "Shirley, hold my calls until I tell you different. Okay?"

Once inside and seated, JJ unloaded his concerns and rage over Little Bob's brutal attack on the three young Hispanic boys, and what legal charges, if any, could be implemented. The discussion continued with "back and forth" opinions and both in agreement that Little Bob had to be held responsible for this outrageous attack.

JJ offered his thanks to the Sheriff with a handshake and departed.

Driving back to the Split Aces, JJ's mind was switching from one scenario to another as to what personal action he should pursue with Little Bob. A personal confrontation would probably not end well, so a phone call would be the best way to handle the situation.

Once he arrived at his ranch, and having decided his next course of action, JJ immediately went to his office. Not even taking time to sit down, he picked up his phone and dialed the Herring Ranch.

Five rings later, he answered. "Little Bob here, what can I do for you?"

"It's JJ, and what you can do is to buy your ticket to hell, cause that's where you're going. And another thing, if you ever touch one of my ranch hands or their children again, I'll punch that ticket for you and I damn sure mean every word I'm saying."

Not waiting for a response, he cradled the receiver, departed, and like Elvis, was no longer in the house.

CHAPTER FIFTY-TWO

The Deer Hunting Trip

It was a typical day for late November, a bit colder than normal, but a bright sun provided adequate warmth for the citizens of Burson as they routinely traveled from store to store in search of advertised bargains offered by the annual Thanksgiving Sale promotions. Bob Bullock's day at the office had been reasonably quiet for most of the day, and he was half-dozing while reclining in his office chair when he bolted to an upright position roused by the sharp ringing of his private telephone line.

"Bullock here," was his immediate response.

"Bob, JJ, what you got going on this beautiful day?"

"Not much, JJ, in fact It's been a real slow day for the banking business, and I was about halfway napping. What you got on your mind?"

"Just caught the weather news on the tube a while ago, and they're predicting a low-forties temperature for the next couple of mornings; so I'm thinking it's high time you and I got out the deer rifles, oiled 'em up and hit the deer lease tomorrow; we just might snag us a couple of good Bucks early the next morning. I thought the timing might be good for you since the Aggies aren't playing this weekend, seeing as how their getting ready for the big Thanksgiving Day game with the Longhorns."

If there was anything in Bob's passion in life that even come close to Texas A&M football, it was deer hunting. He was quick to reply: "JJ, you must be a mind reader; I was just day-dreaming about that big Buck that got away last year. I'll bet my bottom dollar that he's up there just daring us to come after him again."

JJ Stephens voice, crackled because of age and too excessive yelling at cows and other livestock over a period of many years, seemed almost musical as he replied, "Dang it, Bob, that sounds good to me. I just rode that southern section out this morning looking for stray calves, and the signs are all there, deer tracks and droppings all over the place. Haven't seen too many with my own eyes, but you know, they feed early and late, and I'll guarantee we got a lot of them out there this year. What do you say? Are we a go?"

"Sure thing, count me in. By the way, I've been doing a little thinking and have a suggestion to offer, that is, if you don't bite my head off when I tell you my idea."

JJ had a bit of anxiety in his voice as he spoke, "I'm all ears, let's hear it."

"Well, you know that Melba's been on my back for years about our hunting trips. Seems as though she doesn't understand how we can enjoy just sitting out in the cold waiting for some big old Buck to wander into our view so we can do-pop him. So, I've been promising her for some time now that one day I'll let her tag along and show her how really relaxing it is, and just how much fun we do have." And, Bob paused in the middle of his sentence as his mind was searching for the next thing to say without causing an outburst from his close friend for many years, he continued, "Well, it sure as hell ain't no secret that you and my gal Maggie have got a little thing going for several years now, although you neither one say much about it. Understand, it's none of my business, but I was thinking this would be a good time for me to take Melba and maybe you could invite Maggie to go along. I could have Melba call her and set things up. You got your camper and I got that little pop-up trailer that we could pull along. The girls could bunk in the nice one and you and I could take the pop-up and get along just dandy, and we got the sleeping bags, so we'll be warm enough. Sort of introduce the girls to the outdoor life, what do you think?"

"Just for your info, Bob, Maggie, and I are just friends; nothing real serious going on here. We share a dinner date every now and then, an occasional movie, and she's had me over for dinner a few times. But we've never talked about anything long term, and don't suspect we ever will. She's a real nice lady, and I respect her and enjoy her company, and for now, I'd like to keep it that way."

"No skin off my nose either way, I wasn't trying to play cupid, just wanted to get Melba out to the lease one time and came with the idea about Maggie. I know Melba and Maggie get along real good, and I think we would all have a good time. We could probably get in a little poker game in the down time, and the girls could sure help with the cooking. That cooking out has never been my strong suit, and after all these years of you and I hunting together, I know dang well, it's sure not your strong suit either."

JJ laughing replied, "One thing is, you may not have liked my cooking, but you dang sure didn't lose any weight on my watch."

Both men, long-time friends, enjoyed the lighter moments of their conversation.

Bob continued, "Let's just get it done. I'll talk to Melba and you talk to Maggie. Later on Melba and Maggie can work out the food details. That will save us a lot of headaches of shopping. Why don't we throw in a couple more rifles, and we might just give the gals a lesson in shooting? Hell, who knows, they might get to enjoying this hunting business and turn out to be female protégés of Daniel Boone."

JJ, although apprehensive about sharing the proposed outing with the girls, reluctantly agreed to Bob's idea. After wrapping up a few of the details, the conversation ended and both men went about their business preparing for the weekend trip.

Chapter Fifty-Three

Preparation for the Trip

By 10:00 Saturday morning, Bob, Melba, JJ, and Maggie had all agreed to the hunting trip and each in their own way were hard at work preparing for a noon departure. Bob was hustling about cleaning out the pop-up trailer that had not been used since last winter, loading his pickup with sleeping bags, rifles, ammo, lanterns, tools, and an assortment of miscellaneous items that he absolutely deemed to be necessary for a good campout.

Melba and Maggie had discussed the food that would be required, which was quite a different variety than the boys were used to packing for their excursion and had agreed to meet at the local Safeway grocery and market to purchase all the fixings for the weekend. The boys had always carried an ample supply of broiling steaks and baking potatoes for their cookouts, so the girls were pleased to comply with that menu, provided the men did the cooking. The two girls had tentatively planned to provide canned chili, canned beans, some fruit, and a few chocolate bars for dinner, but the offer of the men doing the cooking clearly caught their attention and they were quick to accept the offer of the men assuming the role of camp cooks. Coffee, bacon and eggs and pan-fried toast would suffice for breakfast. The girls obviously were planning a much simpler menu than the boys, who were used to roughing it out, were expecting. It was becoming quite clear to the ladies that a deer hunt was more than just hunting, lots of good food and cold beer was a major part of the expedition.

Only a few minutes past twelve noon, Bob, Melba and Maggie all loaded into his well packed Chevy pickup, pop-up tent trailer in tow, and began the eighteen-mile journey to the Split Aces Ranch, where JJ Stephens was putting the finishing touches on his own packing problems. JJ spotted the group approaching before they had exited the county road onto the approximately one-quarter-mile gravel driveway up to the ranch house itself. A small cloud of dust followed the Chevy and trailer as it pulled into the circular driveway in front of the main house. JJ was standing between the house and a large barn to the right of the house and motioned for Bob to pull into the side of his pickup and trailer parked under a stately live oak that towered over the lot and part of the barn.

While removing his always present Stetson hat, he bowed from the waist and greeted his hunting companions with a big smile and loudly welcomed them. "Howdy, friends, welcome to the Split Aces, famous for hospitality and wild game hunting extraordinaire." Handshakes and hugs followed as the threesome climbed out of the Chevy and eagerly exchanged small talk with their host.

JJ interrupted the ongoing chatter, "Melba and Maggie, Bob's been here dozens of times and knows the campsite we're going to; but just so you know, I'll fill you in with a little of the details. The campsite and deer blinds are on what we call the southern section. No roads, just trails, so the ride will be a bit rough. It's only about twelve miles away, but it will seem like forty, 'cause we got some pretty rough country to drive over and pulling these trailers over that stuff ain't no picnic. However, once we're there, you not gonna believe your eyes. The scenery at the site is magnificent, a pure product of God's making. I can't wait for you to see the sunrise . . . breathtaking."

Bob, nodding in agreement. "Amen to that, JJ. You'll see, girls, the cowboy doesn't lie. We're all set here, JJ, what about you?"

"Ready as ready can be, let's load 'em up and head 'em out. Maggie, get your butt in my pickup and we'll lead the way. Bob, you and Melba can ride drag."

ature

CHAPTER FIFTY-FOUR

The Trip Begins

JJ's off-the-cuff remark about the twelve-mile journey seeming like forty was not only poetic, but also grossly understated. The actual arrival time at the campsite, confirmed by the well-organized Maggie Jones with the aid of her reliable Bulova, was five minutes over one hour from time of departure. Maggie made sure that JJ knew exactly how much longer it had taken than he had indicated. The good-natured ribbing between the two friends was accepted and welcomed.

An open fireplace was still in good shape from the previous years of use. Sandstones in a circle and ashes from previous fires made up the open fire pit. The stack of firewood was close at hand but drastically depleted and would have to be replenished. Searching for dry wood would fall under Bob and JJ's job description. True back-wood campers usually cooked by placing the skillet, coffee pot etc. directly on the hot coals and ashes from the firewood. However, after years of accidently dumping several pots of coffee and overturning several skillets of food, Bob had purchased a heavy steel wire grill to rest on the sandstones surrounding the pit. That had provided a much more stable cooking platform and significantly reduced the amount of cooking incidents.

After pointing out the rocks and foliage identified as the ladies restroom, opposite from the huge boulders the boys would use, JJ and Bob set out to search for firewood as the girls decided to heed nature's call at their private restroom behind the designated rocks. Later, when all the camp prep had been completed, the four friends settled into four folding lawn chairs surrounding a small campfire and enjoyed sandwiches, chips, cold beer, and soda all prepared and served by Melba and Maggie.

JJ, at first reluctant to have the two girls accompany he and Bob on this trip, at last was beginning to see the benefit of their presence. Not a bad idea, Bob Bullock, not a bad idea at all.

After the late lunch and bit more of organizing of the campground and stabilizing the campers for the night's use, Bob announced to the ladies, "Okay, Melba and Maggie, it's time you took a little shooting practice." He then rambled over to the pickup, opened the backdoor and picked up two rifles both contained in canvas gun bags. Returning to the campfire he handed one to Melba and the other to Maggie.

JJ pulled himself out of his camp chair and approached Maggie. "Hey Mag, let me give you a hand with that."

Maggie, with a bit of sarcasm in her voice, replied, "Girls may not be great hunters JJ, but it doesn't take much brains or skill to open a zipper. I do believe I can handle this by myself."

"Now don't get all touchy on me, I was just gonna help you with the rifle, not the case."

In a softer and gentler voice, "In that case, thank you. I rescind my smart-ass remark . . . my apology."

"No apology required; It's all-in good fun."

Turning to Bullock, "Hey Bob, what did you bring the ladies for shooting?"

Bullock was returning from a second trip to his pickup carrying a beautifully engraved leather rifle case and responded, "l brought a couple of Remington Mohawk 600s, one is a .243 and the other is a .222. I thought I'd let Melba shoot the smaller caliber since she's a bit more petite than Maggie. Let Maggie try the .243. After a few practice shots, they'll both be okay with them."

The rifles that Bob Bullock had furnished for Melba and Maggie were Remington Model 600 Mohawk short-barreled deer rifles with minimum recoil, ideal for women, younger hunters, and gun collectors. Bob, an avid hunter, had enough rifles in his collection to supply a small army. Although he protected them in secure rifle vaults, he was more than generous in loaning rifles to friends for hunting excursions. His personal rifle of choice for this trip was a top-of-the-line Weatherby Mark V, chambered for 300 Weatherby mag. He usually saved this rifle for special occasions, so at least in his mind, this was that kind of an occasion.

JJ had produced his own weapon of choice, his trusted Winchester Model 70, a 30.06 caliber, that he had purchased years ago and with which he had bagged many a trophy buck, whose antlers now adorned his ranch house den wall.

JJ reached over and grabbed Maggie by the hand, gently pulled her to her feet, and begin walking away from the campsite.

"Where to?" questioned Maggie.

"Everyone, follow me," JJ replied as he playfully tugged her along a trail.

Bob and Melba, with rifles in hand, followed JJ's lead. About two hundred yards down the trail, a generous clearing emerged, and JJ signaled this was the spot where the shooting lesson would begin. From a small tote bag that he had shouldered he retrieved several empty soda cans and carefully arranged them in a row a couple of feet apart. The terrain to their left was up a slight incline and he proceeded to lead the party up the slight hill approximately twenty-five yards before calling the party to a halt.

"This is it, ladies, let the fun begin."

The next several minutes consisted of instructions from A to Z, loading ammo, adjusting scope, safety procedures, proper way to hold the rifle, squeezing the trigger and where to aim for the kill of the buck, provided you were lucky enough to obtain a shot. The plan was to start the practice shots from this distance, and when successful, gradually move to longer distances, more realistic to the actual distance that a shot at a live target would require.

Maggie took the first shot with her .243 and kicked up dirt just in front of the first target.

"Not bad Maggie, not bad at all. Give her a second go."

The second shot was almost perfect for distance, but three inches to the left.

"That's it, gal, just a little more steady. You were wobbling a bit."

Maggie raised the rifle to her shoulder, aimed slightly above the target, and then gradually lowered the barrel until the can came into sight. She squeezed off the round and the impact of the direct hit launched the soda can into the air before landing several feet away tumbling end over end down the incline.

Obviously pleased with her performance, she smilingly turned to her three applauding fellow hunters, "Third time's a charm, as the old saying goes."

It was now Melba's turn, and although she did not have the immediate success that Maggie displayed, she did manage to get a couple of close-range shots to her credit. Forty-five minutes and dozens of shots later, Maggie was deemed the winner of the "Annie Oakley" award and Melba the runner up. Laughter and light banter exchanged between the four friends as they made their way back to the campsite. Later, Maggie would confess that she did have some previous experience with a twenty-two-caliber rifle. As a teen-ager, she had accompanied a friend on a couple of rabbit hunting outings on the ranges of west Texas and had bagged a couple on one trip. However, in her defense, and in her words, "That was a very, very, long time ago, and she had not fired a rifle since those teenage days."

Back at the campsite, a couple of hours rest was next in order, all before late evening when the live hunting action would begin.

Chapter Fifty-Five

A Late-Night Trip to the Emergency Room

Shortly after midnight on a Saturday late in April, a sleek looking black Buick Roadmaster wheeled to a screeching halt under the covered entrance of the Burson General Hospital Emergency Room. Quickly exiting from the driver's side door, and without taking time to close it, Little Bob Herring rushed into the lobby and yelled at the first employee he saw. "I need help real quick like. My wife has had an accident and is bleeding pretty badly. Also, I think we need a wheelchair."

The administrative assistant working the registration desk quickly picked up the intercom mike and forcefully yelled: "Need help in the lobby real pronto."

Not pausing to wait, Little Bob spotted a wheelchair in the corner of the lobby, grabbed it and started out the door furiously pushing it toward his car, engine still running and lights still shining. Inside, reclining against the headrest, Betty Jean, sobbing softly, was holding a blood-soaked towel to her left ear with her right hand, while her left hand lay limply across her lap. Her clothing, a pale pink nightgown

with a matching cotton robe secured loosely with a flannel belt, was equally soiled with the excessive amount of blood draining from her injury. Even the auto's plush upholstery was not spared the wrath of the pathfinding blood trail.

Even before he could attempt to help Betty Jean into the chair, a young, tall, lean attendant was there by his side, "Let me do it, sir. I know how and I can handle it."

"Okay, but please be careful. I don't know how bad she's hurt."

As he continued to comfort her he calmly asked, "Where do you hurt, Ma'am? Is there anything other than your arm and ear?"

Still sobbing softly, she barely whispered in replying, "I'm not sure, but I don't think so."

Patiently, while attempting to ensure that no broken bones would impede her transfer to the wheelchair, He asked: "Can you tell me what happened?"

Hesitantly, she paused for a moment, and then in a barely audible voice: "I . . . I think I fell down our stairs, but, but uh, l must have blacked out because I can't, uh, remember much about what happened."

After a thorough examination by the ER doctor on staff, it was determined that other than a couple of broken ribs and severe bruising, the patient had no life-threatening complications due to the accident she had suffered. The bleeding from her ear was probably due to bumping her head as she fell. After a sedative had been applied she drifted off into a good night's sleep, and only awakened the following morning when the nurse on duty gently shook her shoulder to help with her breakfast tray.

"Emily Jean and Brenda Kaye, where are they? Are they okay, where is Little Bob?"

Nurse JoAnn, "Mr. Herring called early this morning and asked me to inform you that he would pick up the girls from his mother and dad and bring them to the hospital shortly after they had their breakfast. He spent most of the night at your bed side and only left this morning. He seemed to be extremely concerned about your physical condition."

Chapter Fifty-Six

What Really Happened the Previous Night?

After a 6:00 p.m. dinner and Betty Jean had finished putting all the dishes in the dishwasher, cleaned the table and placed all the leftovers in the fridge, she walked up the stairs and helped her precious daughters with their pajamas and tucked them into bed. Only after the goodnight kisses and the assurance that the girls were down for the night that she went downstairs to the den, fell into her favorite lounge chair, and picked up the novel that she had been reading for the last couple of days.

Meanwhile, Little Bob was busy pouring himself one glass of Jack Daniels after another, seemingly intent on drinking enough to drown himself into a drunken stupor. A couple of hours later, Betty Jean put down her book, rose from her chair, and walked over to the chair where Little Bob was sitting, kissed him lightly on the cheek and told him of her intentions to go to bed. But as she turned to go up the stairs, he grabbed her by the arm and roughly pushed her into the adjoining chair. In a voice too loud and garbled, like anyone who has had too much to drink, he insisted she listen to what he had to say. "I guess you think that I don't know what's going on with you and your little fling. Think I'm just too busy working or too damn dumb to know that you and your old boyfriend are screwing around behind my back."

"What in the world are you talking about?" she practically shouted. "Dang sure have not been with anyone since I married you, and sure as hell have not been involved with Parker, whom I presume you were talking about as an old boyfriend." With a trembling voice, she continued, "And as far as that little subject goes, I have not hidden the fact that I occasionally drop by his office, not to see him, but because of all the years I worked there, I developed a strong friendship with all of the office employees and enjoy keeping in contact with them. And besides that, Mary Francis, the secretary that took my place, and I have also become friends. And to conclude this little conversation, I do sometimes visit with Parker, whom I have never seen drunk, unlike someone I know, and is too much of a gentleman to ever make a pass with a married lady."

She pushed herself from her chair and started for the stairway leading to her bedroom. Pausing at the first step, she turned and faced her unusually quiet and dumbfounded husband, who had not uttered a word during her total rejection of his aforementioned accusation of infidelity. "You're drunk. Go to bed and sleep it off." That being said, and with no rebuttal from her husband, she continued up the stairway.

Still weeping crocodile size tears from the downstairs accusation from her husband that she had been unfaithful to him, she managed to remove her makeup, wash her face, brush her teeth, and slip into her gown and robe, and headed for her bedroom. As she entered the room, her husband was standing near the bed, totally inebriated, and swaying from side to side trying to keep his balance.

"Hey Babe, if you think little conversation is over, you sure as hell got another thing coming, 'cause I damn sure got a lot more to get off my chest. If you think I'm buying that story about you just visiting your totty-totty friends down at Parker's office, you can just throw that in that pile of fiction books you read." Almost falling, he staggered to the edge of the bed and sat down.

Not wanting to go to bed with her husband still ranting and reeling, she sat down in one of the chairs near the bed and decided that the best course of action for her was to hear him out.

After a few minutes of neither of the two speaking and Little Bob attempting to clear his head, she cleared her thoughts and in a calm voice, "Honey, you have had way too much to drink and you are not in a condition to talk about this rationally, so why don't you get ready for bed and we will discuss this tomorrow after we both have had a night to rest?"

A few minutes passed with neither one speaking nor noticeably moving about, Betty Jean stood up and quietly announced, "Please get ready for bed, we both need the rest and will both benefit from a good nights' sleep."

"No," he angerly shouted. "You are going to hear this now. I know a whole lot more than you know that I know. It just so happens that at least two times, you were with your old boyfriend, Mr. Parker himself. If your memory needs updating, about six months after Emily was born, you left her with my mom and dad while you went to Abilene on a so-called shopping trip. Just so happens, that I decided to have a little business meeting with Parker. Mary Francis informed me that Parker was going out of town on a business trip and would be unavailable for the rest of the day. About six weeks later, same song, same verse, Mr. Parker not available, out of town on a business trip and unavailable for the rest of the day. And now that I've thought it out, Brenda Kaye's daddy is probably Parker, cause she damn sure don't look like Emily Jean."

Now trembling and crying from both anger and resentment she almost shouted the words, "That's enough, you are making a fool out of yourself. I'm going downstairs and make some coffee and try to sober you up."

Taking the first three or four steps, she turned to see Little Bob frantically trying to catch up with her as she continued to descend the stairway. Turning to confront him, she almost yelled in his face, "Leave me alone, I've had enough of your insults for one night. Get over it, the coffee will be ready in about ten minutes."

His anger was increasing by the seconds as he grabbed her by the arm and pulled her toward his body. Now totally out of patience and fearful of what he might do to her physically, she tried to free her arm from his grip, but he was much stronger and tightened his grip even more, digging his fingernails into her skin as the blood began to ooze into her nightgown. Panic-stricken, she used her free hand and slapped him solidly in the face. Now totally out of control, and not thinking rationally, he lashed back with a fist to the side of her face, and in so doing, lost his balance, pulling her with him as they tumbled together down the remaining three or four steps.

For several minutes, they both lay together on the floor near the staircase. Rising to a sitting position, he quietly looked around and tried to clear his mind as to what had just happened. Softly crying, and in obvious pain, Betty Jean was now bleeding from the ear and shaking as she laid on the floor in a cramped position.

"My *God,* what have I done? Betty Jean, Betty Jean, where do you hurt; did you break any bones? Oh my God, I'm so sorry. I did not mean to hurt you. My God, I was such a fool. I've got to get you to the hospital. Can you sit up? Here, let me help you."

In the following minutes, he telephoned his parents and told them Betty Jean had fallen down the stairs and was in great pain. Would they please come over and stay with the girls, as he was leaving to take her to the emergency room. He quickly brought the Buick to the front door and carefully helped lift her in the front passenger seat. The trip to the hospital was underway.

The Suffering is Finally Over

Shortly before 4:00 a.m., Sunday May 4th, 1980, Bob Bullock's Dodge Ram one-half ton pickup pulled out of his private parking place in the small back parking lot in the rear of the Burson National Bank. After a right turn on Third Street and a short drive to Main, and without the use of headlights, the driver turned left and slowly headed east on State Hwy 380. The city lights, only two per block, provided ample vision for the driver to safely navigate the unoccupied street. Without racing the engine, the driver was attempting to depart the city without being noticed. No one was up and around in the business sector, and once it approached the sparsely inhabited entrance to the downtown section, the driver switched on the headlights and accelerated to a near normal speed limit.

Less than five minutes later, and with a slight mist filling the air, the Dodge pickup slowed to a crawl, and abruptly turned right onto a seldom used dirt road, the entrance to old Herring Ranch House. And after switching the headlights off, and again navigating in a very dark setting, the sole occupant backed and maneuvered the pickup into an area between the trees where it was partially concealed from view. After retrieving a thirty-caliber Winchester Deer rifle from the storage area behind the seat, the mysterious driver chambered a thirty-caliber shell and double checked the weapon to ensure the weapon was ready to fire, the soon-to-be assailant started the approximately five-hundred-yard walk toward the Bob Herring Jr. home.

Agilely weaving in and around native brush and trees the assailant quickly reached a destination that, while offering concealment, also, presented a perfect view of the Herrings' spacious back porch. The live oak that offered cover was native and having not been pruned had several low branches, perfect height for resting a rifle. Now only the seemingly endless waiting period was to be overcome.

Bob Jr. was known, by anyone that had engaged him in meaningful conversation, to be an early riser and enjoyed his early morning cup of coffee while sitting on his back porch. This Sunday morning was no exception. Clad only in pajama bottoms, house shoes, and a lightweight windbreaker, Little Bob emerged from the kitchen with coffee in hand. Leaning on one of the supporting posts to the porch, his eyes randomly gazed out over the tree covered pasture into the gradual lighting of the eastern sky. Often, early in the morning or late in the evening, it was not unusual to spot deer grazing on the rich range grass near his home. Only for a moment, after a slight movement to his left caught his eye, he attempted to fix his gaze on that object, hoping to catch a glimpse of the big buck that freely roamed his pasture. It was not the big Buck deer that had entered his path of vision.

The sharp crack of the rifle shot shattered the early morning silence. Bob Herring Jr. probably never heard the sound as the bullet, faster than sound, punctured his chest, a perfect shot from the marksman assailant. He crumpled to the floor of the porch as the still steaming coffee flew from his hand and splattered over the wall and floor. He lay motionless.

Taking only a few seconds to satisfy that the shot had accomplished the mission, the gunman picked up the expended cartridge, pocketed it, and retraced her steps to old Herring Ranch Road where the concealed pickup was parked. Arriving at the pickup, she calmly placed the rifle in the original storage area behind the seat and started to climb behind the wheel. The unexpected sound of an approaching vehicle initiated a quick change of plans. Slamming the cab door shut to extinguish the cab lights, she quickly turned and attempted to disappear into the underbrush. The tail lights of the passing Chevrolet Silverado brightened for a couple of seconds as Chat Cason hit the brake pedal while attempting to identify the unusual parking of the vehicle and the movement surrounding it. A split second later a sickening sound, this time that of crashing steel, but like the gunshot only minutes before, again shattered the early morning silence.

The clock on the Dodge Ram dashboard indicated 5:30 a.m. as Margaret Ann Burke wheeled into the back parking lot of the Burson National Bank. Not even one car or truck had she encountered in the five-minute drive from the Herring Ranch. She calmly parked the Dodge in the original parking place, reserved for Bull, who was out of town for the weekend.

After retrieving the rifle from behind the seat and using Bull's cleaning kit, that when on slow days he often used in his office, she preceded to rod clean the barrel of any residue.

After wiping the rest of the rifle clean of any fingerprints she replaced the rifle to the original place in the pickup behind the seat. Most farm and ranch residents keep a rifle in their pickup because of coyotes and other like animals that endanger their calves, lambs, chickens and such. Assured that no one was watching, she calmly walked to the back door, disabled the alarm, and after resetting it, walked routinely to her office and serviced the coffee maker.

Now, with a couple of hours to reminisce, she could finally feel the satisfaction of taking care of a long-time problem. Although years earlier she had agreed to a pre-adoption clause prohibiting her from ever revealing the relationship between she and her baby daughter, she secretly kept up with her from kindergarten through her college days. And when the vacancy for a secretarial position at Parker Coburn's Company became available, it was she that mailed the newspaper clipping to her daughter, Betty Jean Morrison. To protect her identity and her relationship, she purposely removed the return address to make it appear to have been damaged in the mail.

Although extremely disappointed in her daughter's marriage to Little Bob Herring and knowing his past problems, she nevertheless said anything negative about, that only she knew to be, her son-in-law. Only when the physical abuse became more evident, that she decided to take whatever action was required to solve the problem and protect her daughter and grandchildren.

Not eavesdropping but just listening to her boss's unnaturally low, almost whispering, phone conversation with other members of the Friday Five, she suspected that some plans were being talked about to take care of the problem. She later realized it might be something drastic. If she took care of the problem, neither her boss nor any of the others of the Friday Five, all of whom she loved like brothers, could ever be charged. By keeping her secret, that she was Betty Jean's mother, no one would ever know that it was she that pulled the trigger.

Several times in the past, she had stopped by the office before attending Sunday school at the First Baptist Church. The bathroom was available for a leisure clean-up, church-going clothes had been previously hidden in her private office closet, and a package of cinnamon rolls purchased at the local bakery Friday, were still fresh enough for breakfast. Her office was even furnished with a soft couch for occasional rest, a gift from Bob Bullock, during hours of overtime work. Nothing out of the ordinary was occurring when at nine o'clock sharp, she departed for the ten-block drive to the First Baptist Church. Margaret Ann was not one to take Sunday school and Church attendance lightly.

The suffering is finally over.

Author's Note: I, along with you, will always wonder, who drew the two?

About the Author

Melton, born in Eastland County Texas in October 1928. As the only child of John and Allie Luttrell, Melton grew up in the small town of Caddo, ninety miles west of Fort Worth, Texas. Melton's father only had a second-grade education, and being the eldest of five siblings, had to drop out of school and take over his father's work who had suffered a permanent disability injury. Using the team of mules that led the wagon that they lived in as sharecroppers, he earned money by dragging cut-down trees to clear the valley for construction of the dam that would become Lake Cisco. He continued to be the "breadwinner" for his family until his siblings were old enough to assume that responsibility.

Later John became a self-taught mechanic, and opened a business of his own: a service station and auto mechanic garage. Obviously, Melton had all the love of his parents, but also from a very young age was taught that work came with the territory. Every summer, thinking that school was over and that summer would be filled with swimming and playtime, he was disappointed when his father would say, "Go see Mr. Garvin or Mr. Hudspeth. They have a job for you." Later in life, Melton realized the value of his father's teachings.

After attending John Tarleton Junior College, Melton worked as a maintenance electrician for Texas Electric. While living in Ranger, Texas, it was there that he met the love of his life, that later in November 1949, became his wife, until her pass- ing on to a higher place after almost seventy years of marriage. It was she, Susia Mae Caraway, that tricked him into taking Square Dancing lessons, something he had previously refused to do, thinking that was not the kind of dancing he enjoyed. Not only did he enjoy the lessons, weekly for ten weeks, and only two months into the lessons he was asked to become a caller by one of the students, Judge C.B. Long, who, like being a Godfather, paid his expenses to attend Herb Greggerson's Caller's school in Ruidosa, New Mexico.

Following World War Two, Square Dancing was booming and Melton was soon working several nights per month and making a decent second job income. After much discussion, Sue, as Susia was best known, and Melton agreed that the smartest thing they could do was to move somewhere that he could con- tinue his education and achieve a college degree. In 1953, they loaded their sons, their dog, and what they could pile into their Pontiac coupe and headed to Fort Worth, Texas to start a new chapter in their life.

Working at various daytime jobs and some nights of Square Dancing, Melton attended night school at Texas Christian University, and in 1959 was awarded a bachelor's degree in Mathematics. He was a longtime employee, more than thirty-seven years, retiring from Lockheed-Martin in 1996.

Melton also recorded several records for Square-L-Records, which he organized and managed for several years.

Beginning in 1960, Melton and Sue managed several Square-L Records Institutes annually at various resorts in New Mexico, Oklahoma, and Texas. They also were staff members at yearly Square Dance resorts in Colorado and Missouri. Melton has called festivals in over forty states and abroad in England, Australia, New Zealand—and even Saudi Arabia.

A supporting and charter member of Callerlab, the International Association of Square Dance Callers, Melton served as a member of the Board of Governors from 1972 until 1997.

Melton designed, built, and managed Swingtime Center, one of the nation's finest Square Dance facilities and was instrumental in the organization of CASUL, Inc. that now owns and operates Swingtime Center. He served as their president for the first five years, and still remains on the board today.

He was inducted into the American Square Dance Hall of Fame in 1977, he was awarded Callerlab's Milestone award, the highest recognition of achievement in 1986. He was inducted into the North Texas Callers Hall of Fame in 1998, and the Texas Callers Hall of fame in 2008.

Although Square Dancing remains a principal part of his life, Melton's family of two sons, six grandchildren, and sixteen great-grandchildren now receive an increasing amount of his time. A second book, provided the first is reasonably received, is a strong possibility.